THE QUENTARIS CHRONICLES

Quentaris in Flames, Michael Pryor
Swords of Quentaris, Paul Collins
The Perfect Princess, Jenny Pausacker
The Revognase, Lucy Sussex
Beneath Quentaris, Michael Pryor
Slaves of Quentaris, Paul Collins
Stones of Quentaris, Michael Pryor
Dragonlords of Quentaris, Paul Collins
Angel Fever, Isobelle Carmody
The Ancient Hero, Sean McMullen
The Mind Master, John Heffernan
Treasure Hunters of Quentaris, Margo Lanagan
Rifts through Quentaris, Karen R. Brooks
The Plague of Quentaris, Gary Crew
The Cat Dreamer, Isobelle Carmody
Princess of Shadows, Paul Collins
Nightmare in Quentaris, Michael Pryor
The Murderers' Apprentice, Pamela Freeman

The Cat Dreamer

Isobelle Carmody

Series editors: Michael Pryor and Paul Collins

For Diane

Thomas C. Lothian Pty Ltd
132 Albert Road, South Melbourne, Victoria 3205
www.lothian.com.au

First published 2005

National Library of Australia
Cataloguing-in-Publication data:

Carmody, Isobelle, 1958–
The Cat Dreamer

ISBN 0 7344 0762 9

I. Title. (Series: Quentaris chronicles).

A823.3

Cover artwork by Marc McBride
Back cover artwork by Grant Gittus
Map by Jeremy Maitland-Smith
Original map by Marc McBride
Cover and text design by John van Loon
Printed in Australia by Griffin Press

Contents

QUENT
THE RIF
THE
BARRENLANDS
13
8
THE
GREA

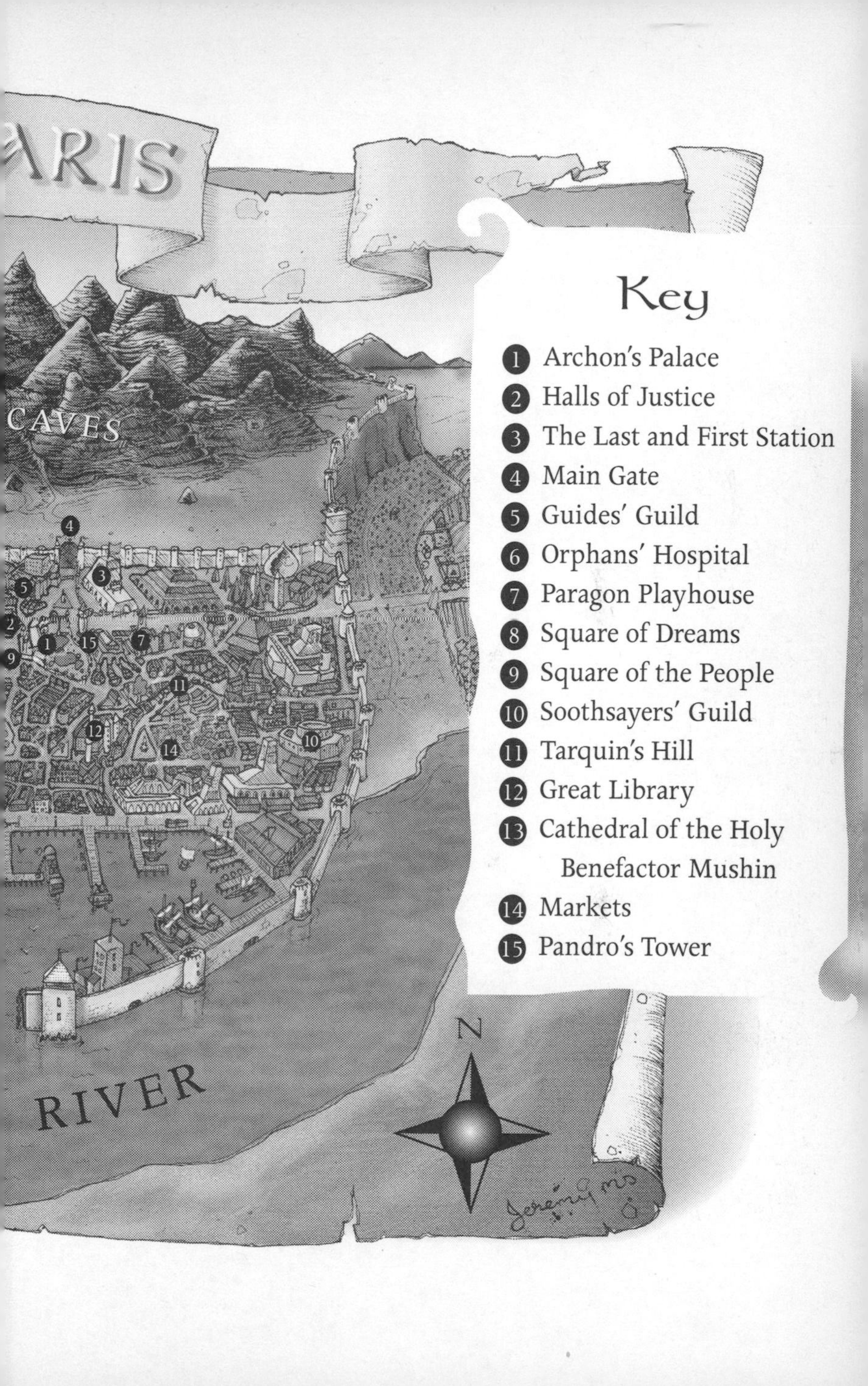
ARIS
CAVES
RIVER
N
Key
1 Archon's Palace
2 Halls of Justice
3 The Last and First Station
4 Main Gate
5 Guides' Guild
6 Orphans' Hospital
7 Paragon Playhouse
8 Square of Dreams
9 Square of the People
10 Soothsayers' Guild
11 Tarquin's Hill
12 Great Library
13 Cathedral of the Holy Benefactor Mushin
14 Markets
15 Pandro's Tower

1

A City Befogged

RED GAZED THROUGH THE window of the cramped Watch hut and sighed. The idea of going out into the damp air and patrolling the long stony stretch of ground before the rift caves every fifteen minutes had been Cora's. It was a matter of pride to her that the Watch assigned to rift guard were alert when she was in charge.

Donning his cloak, Red tried to recall exactly when Cora had issued the order to patrol. It had definitely been since the arrival of the fog that currently shrouded Quentaris, because one of the Watch that had fallen asleep claimed it had confused her into unconsciousness.

And the fog had arrived when? A week ago. Two weeks? Red decided the troll brew his twin brother had pressed on him the night before must have affected his memory. He had no clear recollection of how much he had drunk, but he had ended up being carried to bed, slung like a sack of potatoes over Igorik's shoulder. He ought to have a mighty hangover, but in fact he had awoken rested and clear-headed.

He stepped out into the clammy gloom, reminding himself as one did these days, that it was only late afternoon. The fog had reduced night and day to a queer, shifty dusk. The street lamps were left alight constantly, though their grainy puddles of brightness offered little illumination. Which explained why the streets were deserted. People had no doubt begun to prefer to stay indoors with their curtains drawn until the fog lifted. Though who knew when that would be? It seemed a long time since he had seen a clean blue sky, let alone sunlight.

It occurred to Red as he strode towards the gate in the stone wall that separated the rift caves from the city, that he was noticing the fog more today because he had spent the night in the unfogged subterranean part of Quentaris. He had not noticed before, for instance, how claustrophobic it was to be able to see only a few feet in any direction.

Passing through the gate in the rift wall, he came to a halt, and cast his eyes up to the cliffs which reared above Quentaris. Of course he couldn't see the top now, nor, when he looked sideways, could he see to the other end where most of the bigger caves were situated. Within the multitude of openings, some accessible only by narrow paths zigzagging unevenly up the cliff face, lay the magical rifts which were the source of all Quentaris's cosmopolitan wealth.

He made a cursory inspection of the closest caves. The rifts within the caves allowed access to numerous other worlds for those who dared or had the ability to walk their unstable and potentially treacherous paths, and they also allowed people and creatures from other worlds to come to Quentaris. But most who came were from worlds with established trade links and bound on pursuing their specific ends, or they were utterly bewildered having stumbled on a rift connection in their own world which might or might not be permanent. The members of the Watch on rift duty were supposed to give directions to the purposeful, and usher the lost calmly and firmly to the orientation centre run by the guides. Here visitors could sleep off their journey, bathe, have wounds attended to and converse with those who could communicate. Later, they would be interviewed by city officials and helped to figure out whether they wished to return to their own world immediately, if that was possible, or delay a little to see the sights. The latter was generally suggested by the guides, too, because it gave them a chance to learn more about other worlds.

Inimical arrivals were thankfully uncommon. Even when some creature or person or group did come through bent on wreaking havoc of one kind or another, they were seldom too much for more than a few of the Watch to handle with stun spells, prod sticks and stupefying puffers. Swords were seldom necessary. There were always ten guards assigned to the main gate, and in such weather as this, all but the one assigned to a stretch in the Watch hut remained inside the guard house playing chess, arguing or gambling.

'No unexpected visitors lurking in the shadows,' Red reported to himself. The joke fell flat though, because the fog had a discomfiting way of swallowing all but the nearest sound, leaving his words sounding thin and uneasy. Cora had not specified patrolling the whole width of the rift caves, and so he turned and began to pace back along the wall, reminding himself to check the reservoirs of the lanterns that hung either side of the gates before he finished.

As he turned to retrace his steps again, he found himself trying to remember a significant event in the last week. Was it possible the troll brew could really have affected his mind? The trolls would not have been permitted to sell something actually dangerous. And yet since when were trolls known to be more than grudgingly law abiding?

Red scowled and thought it would be his brother who would be in peril of his life if that brew had done any permanent damage. Accurate recall was one of the things for which members of the Watch were tested. A good memory was not as important to them as to rift guides whose lives and the lives of others often depended upon their ability to remember trails that differed only in the slightest and almost imperceptible degree. Nevertheless, it was an important and necessary tool.

He ought to have refused to drink, knowing that he had an early parade call the next morning, and couldn't understand why he hadn't. Again he strove to bring the previous week into focus, but it was as if he had lived the whole week in a daze of duty, punctuated by bouts of oddly unfocused melancholy lying in his little room in the barracks staring at the ceiling. The more he pondered it, the more troubled he became.

What in the name of Pandro the Uneasy was going on?

If only he had ignored Igorik's summons. But of course he could no more resist a message than Igorik could ignore his instinct to protect his twin. The fifteen minutes between their births that made Igorik the elder had a lot to answer for! When they had been young, Igorik had more than once saved Red from a beating. But he was a man now, and well and truly capable of fending for himself. It was downright humiliating to have his twin brother appearing to check on him like some demented nanny!

This thought restored his equilibrium because Igorik would be the last person to give him anything that would harm him. But if it was not the troll brew affecting his memory, then why couldn't he remember things? Though that was not quite true. He could remember breakfast. Igorik had cooked it, though what he did to food could better be described as murder. How he had managed to turn the eggs purple and that strange rubbery texture in the process of scrambling them was amazing.

Red's grin faded as it struck him how odd it was that he could perfectly remember that breakfast and the rest of this day, but so little before.

Igorik knew he disliked the under city and rarely asked Red to come to Lower Quentaris. Which was why Red had gone straight to see him the minute he had finished duty the previous night. He had guessed Igorik's note was the result of yet another premonition and meant to stay only long enough to reassure him. But when he tried to leave, Igorik had produced the troll brew.

Red frowned, wondering suddenly if his overprotective brother had laced the brew with wakewell elixir; the latest specialty being touted by the potion peddlers. Certainly Igorik had seemed a lot less concerned about his safety over breakfast, and had made no objection to Red leaving.

'If I was in so much danger, how come you sent a message instead of coming after me?' Red had demanded as Igorik dished them both plates of the vile-looking egg.

Igorik merely answered that he had sensed the danger would be greater if he went to Upper Quentaris. Red forbore to mention that his own twin sense was a lot less detailed when it alerted him that Igorik was in trouble, knowing this would only elicit the lofty assertion that this was because he was *younger*.

Red had departed, ruefully aware that he would be late to report at the barracks because of the time it would take him to negotiate the labyrinthine streets of Lower Quentaris. There were many routes up out of the older sunken part of the city, but most were filthy and would require climbing when he would have no time to change. He had to take one of the few wide, well-lit passages situated some way from Igorik's hovel and the barracks. Fortunately, he had not been hauled over the coals for being out of the barracks a full night because he had managed to slip into the parade call unnoticed while Cora ranted about other absences. A night away tended to be overlooked so long as it didn't happen more than once in a while and as long as you did not turn up falling down drunk for duty. Or late.

He tried again to recall when the fog had come. There had been a lot of complaints and grumbling when it showed no sign of abating after a day or two. The Archon had issued a decree to say that one of the magicians would deal with it. What had happened about that? Red was sure he would have remembered if anything had been tried and had failed. Perhaps the whole thing was still being discussed. Maybe the Archon had offended the magicians, who were now being difficult. Or maybe they were demanding some price or concession the Archon didn't want to pay.

Red was glad his job merely involved dealing with Cora who aside from a recent and unusual bout of melancholy was normally very easygoing. Without warning, a face swam into his thoughts; vividly alive with a pointed chin below steady, determined eyes and a wide firm mouth, all framed in a mass of spiky dark hair. An attractive if rather wilful face.

Iakas.

He smiled and said the young roofie leader's name aloud, savouring the churning warmth it roused. Then he remembered. She had asked him to celebrate her name day, offering the invitation awkwardly, flushing and refusing to look at him. Without waiting for his answer, she muttered that she had to go, and scaled the nearest wall with the casual grace she always exhibited above ground. His heart had done a wild war dance as he watched her ascend, because no matter how casually proffered, the invitation meant a lot. He had all but floated off to duty, imagining that when he arrived at her roost atop the very highest tower of the Soothsayers' Guild house, he would find her alone.

A queasy feeling invaded Red, because the invitation had been made the same day that the fog had come. He had been on duty, daydreaming about being alone with her, when Gar had rushed in shouting that the mother of all fogs was rolling in. That had been more than seven days ago, but Iakas had said her name day was seven days hence.

He must have missed the day.

He felt sick and wondered if he could have some exotic illness that involved loss of memory. After all a forgetting sickness was no stranger than other plagues Quentaris had endured. Once there had been a plague in which half the people in Quentaris had spat out frogs when they spoke, while others had spat coins. Then there had been the time that all women had fallen into an enchanted sleep for a day. Some men claimed it hadn't been long enough, though not within the hearing of their women.

He would visit her tonight after work. Better pick up some moodsweet enchanted chocolates from the market on the way. The trouble was that with Iakas's temper, she was just as likely to throw them at his head before they got a chance to have a softening effect. And how to convince her he had a forgetting sickness, anyway, when he couldn't convince himself?

Yet the fact remained that he *had* forgotten.

Red was in the process of closing the lid of the lantern he had just filled with oil when he noticed a small grey cat sitting on the wall, its pale golden eyes fixed on him. It had no red owner disc. Stray cats had been recently banned from the city, supposedly to keep the streets clean. But everyone knew it was because a soothsayer had told the Archon that the next one which crossed his path would have the power to bring about the end of Quentaris. The Archon was one of those people who thought they could thwart prophecies, and he had even appointed a crew to round up stray cats and transport them beyond the city limits. It did not seem to have occurred to the Archon that they could simply find their way back.

'All of which means that you, puss, are an illegal feline,' Red told the little grey cat. It yawned insolently, displaying a tiny pink tongue and showed no sign of wanting to move. Red held out a big hand, half expecting it to spring away. But it merely sniffed him politely without taking its eyes from his face. Closer, Red saw that its eyes were not grey but slashed and sprinkled with gold. It must be some exotic breed. It was a pretty thing, and he wondered if Iakas would like a cat.

He heard a footfall and swung round, expecting to see Cora, but to his astonishment, it was Igorik.

'What are *you* doing here?' His twin gave him a long-suffering look and he rolled his eyes in disbelief. 'Not another premonition?'

Igorik scowled at the cat. 'That thing is probably full of fleas. And it doesn't have an owner disc.'

Red ignored this, knowing that Igorik disliked cats. 'I'm not in any danger. I told you that this morning.'

His brother ran his fingers through his hair. 'Sometimes this twin thing drives me crazy.'

Red continued stroking the cat remembering only too vividly the period when Igorik had tried to shut him out. It had been extremely painful for both of them, and entirely unsuccessful. Stubborn Igorik had persisted until he had discovered that the connection between twins was a powerful form of natural magic and virtually impossible to disrupt, short of the death of one or both parties. And even that was not certain.

'Are you patting an unregistered cat?'

It was Cora's voice. Red straightened abruptly, aware that he was likely to be confined to barracks for a sevenday if he was lucky. 'I was just ...' he began.

'Grab the blasted thing!' Cora roared, but at that moment the cat erupted, diving between Red and Igorik and managing to scratch both of them with razor-sharp claws before disappearing into the swirling fog.

2

A Curious Cat

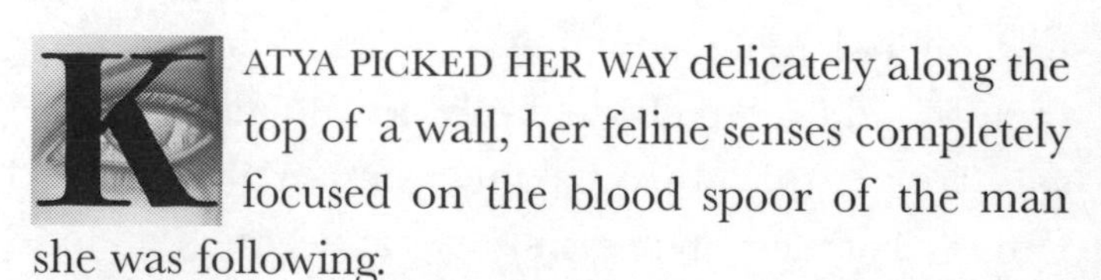

KATYA PICKED HER WAY delicately along the top of a wall, her feline senses completely focused on the blood spoor of the man she was following.

For most shape-changers, assumption of the animal form disabled the human instincts. But for Katya this wasn't so. Her human self did not need dominance to be active, and so while her cat self tracked the man, she considered her impulse to follow him rather than the first man who had smelled of officialdom and the sorts of knowledge and connections she would need.

Her superiors on Astariah viewed the human form as morally and rationally superior. She regarded both parts of her nature as complementary. Each had gifts and disadvantages and whichever could better deal with a situation naturally took control. This did not stop her being able to draw on the abilities of the passive form however. To regard one form as better than another seemed to her as foolish and limited as to prefer your hands to your feet. Each had their unique and irreplaceable purpose.

She sighed, suddenly weary of an argument she had offered too many times to other agents and friends and eventually, foolishly, to her superiors. It was ironic that this balance between her two natures had seen her dismissed, as well as offered this assignment.

When they summoned her, Katya hid her reactions behind a bland mask, determined not to let her superiors see how desperately she wanted to be reinstated. She had seen at once from their faces that there had been no shift in their attitude towards her, and her initial thought had been that they must be offering her a suicide mission.

When they told her the mission required an agent capable of remaining indefinitely in animal form, she had understood. No shape-changer with human dominance would be capable of this. They had no choice but to use her. Yet what could be so important that they would use one of whom they so strongly disapproved? When she asked, they showed her tragic Caris.

Gazing at the near deserted streets of one after another city on Caris she had noted the desolate faces of the few remaining inhabitants. She did not know what had happened to this world, but while human reason spoke of catastrophe, it was her cat nature that understood the deepest truth about what she was being shown. It understood as her human self could not, that all things are interconnected in a world, and when something occurs to shift the balance from striving-to-life to falling-to-death, nothing ultimately would resist. Caris was not dead, but it soon would be …

'Astariah is morally responsible for this crime,' she had been told gravely, sorrowfully. For once

Katya had not experienced the slightest urge to mock the ponderous seriousness of her superior.

'Who did this and how?' she asked with a black kind of marvelling, for it was no small thing to change the balance of life on a world.

'We have named him the Scourge. We do not know precisely how he did this, but we believe it relates to unnatural appetites he … developed here on Astariah some seventy years ago. There were a number of suicides among fellow students for which it was whispered he was responsible. Just before an investigation was due to begin, he vanished. At that time, we were deep in the midst of the closed world debate and so no effort was made to pursue him. No more thought was given to him until the agency began receiving whispers that Caris was foundering. Agents were sent to investigate what seemed such a monstrous rumour we could not believe it to be true. We found Caris as you have seen it. It took some time for our agents to discover that the Scourge had travelled there when he left Astariah, and had been pursuing his activities ever since.'

'And these activities?' Katya had asked.

'It is not necessary that you know their nature. Our wish is merely that you locate this shape-changer and his cell of followers. You will return with the information of their exact location and other agents will be sent to capture them. It is *essential* that the Scourge does not know you are following him, for he will certainly flee. This means you must not, under any circumstances, take your human form.'

'Where did the Scourge and his followers go, for I assume they are not on Caris now?'

'He and his minions escaped through a small, single-person portal on Caris which connects to another world called Ghast where humans are dominant. Of course he knew we would follow once the enormity of the crime on Caris was understood, and again he was prepared. For a time each agent sent was immediately slain. At least we must assume that, for none ever came back to tell their tale. We began seeking out other connections, but we continued to send agents. We had no choice. At last, an agent returned. She had not been killed because the Scourge and his followers had departed. This time, they had travelled through a portal which brought them to a world containing a veritable tangle of portals to a multitude of worlds. Some in the tangle are continuously open and allow trade and travel, such as the one to Ghast, but others open only once, or intermittently, or are extremely difficult to negotiate. The portals lie within a cluster of caves in cliffs that rise above a city called Quentaris, and are controlled by its leaders with the help of guides, but even they have not explored all of the rifts.'

Katya suddenly understood the urgency in the face of her superior. 'The Scourge could use a portal to an unknown world without anyone from Astariah being able to follow him …'

'Not without the aid of a Quentaran guide.'

There was an undercurrent in his tone and Katya, who had never been stupid, understood. 'You think he will remain long enough in Quentaris to master the ability to negotiate these rifts, so that he can travel when and where he likes.'

Her superior cast a swift, pointed glance at his silent colleagues. 'If he does acquire that knowledge, he will inevitably seek to destroy all guides so that we cannot use their knowledge to track him.'

Of course she had accepted the assignment. How could she not? She was told that she must cross through the portals from Astariah to Caris to Ghast and thence transform to cat form to make the final jump to Quentaris. She must seek out the Scourge and gain the knowledge or aid to return to Ghast where a squad of agents would be waiting. Under no circumstance must she alert Quentaris to the danger in their midst lest the Scourge discover Astariah was pursuing him and vanish through one of the countless rifts.

When Katya asked how she was supposed to gain knowledge or information while constantly retaining her animal form, her superior had given her a penetrating look. 'You will observe, of course and if there is no other way, you will enter the mind of any humans able to help you.'

Those words had shocked Katya profoundly.

It was generally believed that only a shape-changer given to beast dominance could enter the mind of another, but this ability was regarded as an abomination and spoken of in whispers. The only shape-changer known to possess it was the infamous and long-dead Rhianna whose beast form had been a tiger. Rhianna had rarely taken her human shape, and had used her power to set up a violent and murderous cult, the eradication of which had necessitated a long bloody war. It was the horrors of that war that had strengthened the prejudice in favour of human minds over beast, but it had also linked the ability to enter minds irrevocably with the evil desire to dominate them.

Katya had discovered quite by chance that *she* could enter other minds, but only when the owner of that mind was sleeping. She had never experienced the slightest desire to control anyone. She had played with dreams, but only those of true felines who never minded and who dreamed while awake as well as while asleep. Katya called her ability *dream merging* and regarded it as no more than a harmless side effect of the balance she had achieved between the two parts of her nature. But she understood that the ability would be deplored as a form of Rhianna's vicious mind domination, and had never used it on any of her own kind, other than twice when she had been on the trail of criminals.

She wished that she had asked how her superiors had learned of her abilities, but at the time, she had been too unnerved by that knowledge to question it.

She asked only one thing and had been given it without question; three days on Caris which she spent in both human and cat forms; prowling, tasting, sensing and reading both papers and the wind; seeking clues about what had happened to Caris; building a scent map of the Scourge. Then she had pronounced herself ready.

As was often the case when she allowed her human mind to wander while seeking an answer to a difficult question, she had come far from the thing that had begun the trail of thought and so, far from an answer.

Her cat self suddenly pointed out with asperity that one did not need to know the *why* of everything. Her cat instincts had compelled her to follow this man and she would learn why soon enough by the doing of it! Her cat persona was less driven by reason than by a highly developed awareness of possibility which bordered on premonition. Of course that could not be understood in human terms.

She stopped, for the man she was following had turned into the doorway of a shabby house. He fumbled with something metallic which human reason told her must be a key, and let himself inside. This was his home then.

Katya surveyed the dwelling with its canting roof and small shuttered windows and thought it a dingy hovel compared to her own white and spacious stone apartment built on a cliff overlooking the jewel-bright sea. She wondered why the human chose to live in this dreary under city. Certainly the streets of the upper city of Quentaris were more beautiful and they were open to the sky and weather. Or would be if it were not for the fog. But perhaps the thick, dirty fog she had noticed upon emerging from the rift caves was a constant feature of this world. In which case it might be drier in these subterranean streets. Even so, this street was considerably narrower than others in the under city and the cobbles had a greasy sheen in the little light which fell from one cracked lamp.

Of course, the human might have some reason for being here other than aesthetics or lack of them, Katya reminded herself. She knew too little of Quentaris to make any judgments yet.

She glanced in either direction along the narrow road then walked fastidiously across to the hovel to sniff at the scent the man had left on the single worn step. She used the blood spoor to focus more vividly. Then she preened a little to smooth her soft grey fur, drew a measured breath and sang an alluring request that the man open the door. Her human senses recognised that humans did not possess the subtlety and discernment of hearing to fully appreciate her singing, but she was shocked when the door was suddenly wrenched open.

'What in the blazes are you doing?' the human shouted. 'Get away from here!'

She flickered her ears in annoyance at his abrasive tone, but he ignored her polite signal and slammed the door shut. She stared at it, human and cat selves concurring that the man was undoubtedly a boor. But still her cat senses insisted that she persist. So she took another breath and sang again. This time her song was an insistence that he open and offer her travellers' hospitality.

The door opened, and the man glowered down at her, emanating scents of fury and frustration. All at once the heat of his anger cooled to puzzlement. 'Aren't you the cat that was on the rift wall with Red?' His scent told her that he did not expect an answer, but cat manners required that she respond, so she miaowed that she needed his help.

'What is it? You're hungry?' His voice was surly, but Katya could smell that he was weakening. She offered a plaintive miaow to say that she *was* hungry as a matter of fact. She did not allow a hint of her doubt that there could be anything hygienic, let alone palatable in such a hovel to enter her tone.

'I don't know how you trailed me here, or why,' the man muttered at last. 'I'll feed you this once, but you're away after you've eaten!' He stomped inside.

Katya settled herself neatly on the step and washed her ears and paws.

The man returned with a bowl of some unfortunate smelling and peculiarly coloured bird egg, and a bowl of milk. Katya ignored the food but the milk had a good creamy nourishing scent. She lapped at it approvingly, feeling smug. She had won the first minor skirmish, whether or not the ill-mannered human knew it.

She was curious about Igorik; the man had been close enough for her to imprint his name. Her interest focused on the fact that he was the twin of the other man whose scent she had sampled. What interested her was not their physical similarity but the strong and viable connection she sensed between them. A connection which she had thought impossible between humans who were unable to mesh with others of their kind or with the world at large.

Her human senses recognised the surge of interest for what it was and she chided herself, knowing all too well how much trouble she had got into in her life for indulging the major vice of cat kind — curiosity.

She had a dangerous and important mission to perform, Katya told herself sternly, and she must not allow feline curiosity to make her forget that!

3

A Body of Sorrow

IGORIK GAZED DOWN AT the face of the dead woman. Even after having been submerged for what must be a full night, there was no mistaking her expression of unimaginable desolation. That and the fact that there was no sign of injury or evidence of struggle told him the woman was another suicide. This month there had been seven, not counting this one.

It was a pathetic and gruesome job getting the body out of the slick drain waters and onto one of the cold, narrow ledges that ran along either side of even the most ancient of the drains snaking under Quentaris. The woman was well made and voluptuous, but death had reduced her to a boneless rag doll whose flesh was heavy and stubbornly awkward. When he was sure that she would not roll back off the edge, Igorik stood and wiped his face on a clean cloth he kept in a sealed bag, reflecting that such deaths offered little dignity. He couldn't help but wonder if the woman would have killed herself if she had envisaged this.

'Dead?' Vrod asked, lumbering along the ledge towards him, his drainer sack flat and empty against his broad back. The troll hadn't bothered to wipe the filth of the drain waters from his face. He couldn't see the point of getting clean until they were finished for the day; his troll senses did not perceive the rank stench of the drains as unpleasant. He knelt and began to go through the woman's pockets but Igorik pushed his hands away.

'Leave her,' he said tersely, although he knew as the troll did, that anything found on a dead body was fair salvage. He straightened the woman's limbs, smoothed her clothes over her limbs and crossed her hands over her chest. Pointless of course, because she would have to be carried out of the drains, but Igorik felt that any death deserved at least a moment of respect.

Sitting back on his heels, he willed his magically enhanced eyesight to its fullest sensitivity and noted how smooth and white the woman's skin was, how fine her gown. Igorik knew little of Quentaran aristocracy, but suspected he was looking at one of them. He wanted to despise this wealthy, well-fed woman for whatever paltry thing had driven her to kill herself, but the look on her face stopped him. The despair in it was too profound.

And who knew what chaos and desperation went on inside the mind, whatever the outward circumstances of a person's life. This thought brought another face up from the depths of his memory, young and narrow but also twisted with despair. He thrust it away from him and got abruptly to his feet.

'See if you can find some identification,' he told the troll. His voice was businesslike now and Vrod went back to rummaging. Igorik turned slightly away to change his drainer slicks for boots, thinking of the other suicides. He had seen two at the salvage depot and both had borne similar expressions to this one. Both had been women, one an older teenager dismissed from the dung brigade and the other a woman who had worked a market stall. As to the rest, he catalogued them by what he had heard; three older women who had eked out livings in menial jobs and two middle-aged men, both of whom had been street flotsam. The only thing all of them had in common until now had been their poverty. He wondered cynically if the affluence of the dead woman would cause those in the Halls of Justice to pay more attention to the sudden rash of suicides.

He scowled, his mood darkening further. After all, what could the authorities do, anyway, about people wanting to kill themselves? What could anyone do?

'No identification,' Vrod finally reported, as he heaved the body onto his massive shoulders.

'It doesn't matter,' Igorik said. Their responsibility as drainers only required that any body found be brought to the depot. One of the healers would determine the cause of death and it would be left to the special investigators attached to the City Watch to try to identify it and to inform the family. Igorik knew the procedure because his father had been an investigator. Neither he nor Red had elected to become investigators, though, because they had promised their heartbroken mother that they would not follow in their father's footsteps after he had been killed. Red had done a lot of soul searching, before he had finally tried for the Watch, deciding this did not constitute breaking his promise. But Igorik had never been fond of rules and laws.

Vrod swung his squat but powerful body up a metal ladder and Igorik followed, avoiding looking up into the dangling face of the dead woman, or down, for he disliked heights. It was a long climb from the drain they had been working to the street level of Lower Quentaris, but fortunately trolls had endurance as well as great strength. The point where they emerged was quite close to the depot so there was no need to run a gauntlet of curious onlookers.

As they entered the drainer depot, Igorik felt a familiar twinge in the bit of his mind connected to his twin brother. He ignored it, wondering what the matter was with him lately. It seemed like the feeling that Red was in danger was constant, and yet Red had been in high spirits at breakfast the morning before and later the same day, when Igorik had been driven to make the trek up to Upper Quentaris.

Vrod lay the body of the woman on a pallet set against the depot wall watched by Povelo. The skeletally-thin, half-human attendant watched disdainfully as the troll sat a bench opposite the desk, leaving his human partner to fill out the paperwork. Igorik could hardly complain since the troll had carried the body out of the drains.

'Another suicide?' Povelo inquired.

'Seems like,' Igorik said. 'Only this one looks wealthy.'

'Salvage?'

Igorik jerked his head at Vrod, who lumbered to the desk and turned out his sack. Two rings, a heavy gold ankle bracelet, a green jade pendant and a single earring all removed while he searched for identification. The attendant made a list, frowning at the single earring.

'No coins?'

Vrod shook his shaggy head, and the attendant gave him a long look. 'You can collect your share of the salvage price once we learn who the woman is and if she was carrying anything else.'

Vrod growled in the back of his throat and Igorik

wondered that the attendant could be stupid enough to anger a troll. 'Look Povelo,' he said with weary patience, 'the woman is wearing an evening gown, paper-thin decorative sandals and no cloak. And she was wearing this jewellery. She was obviously dressed for an occasion in her home, with no need to carry coin.'

Povelo pretended to consider and then shrugged. 'All right, take the bag of salvage along to the pay desk and collect your share.'

Vrod snatched the bag and went down the corridor.

'Why do you provoke him?' Igorik asked, pushing over the report to be signed. 'One of these days he'll turn you inside out.'

Povelo gave a thin smile. 'I don't like trolls.'

Igorik said nothing to that. The enmity between non and half humans was often virulent and inexplicable except to the parties involved. Besides which he was pretty sure he *had* heard the clink of coins when he had been straightening her clothes. He held his tongue, less to protect Vrod than to stop the troll dismantling the depot, thereby causing a whole lot more paperwork.

Outside, the troll handed over his share of the

legal salvage price. Then he reached into his pocket, grinning, to produce a hand full of coins.

'One of these days you are going to get caught,' Igorik warned him.

'Not in this life,' the troll jeered. 'Let's get some ale.'

Igorik shook his head. He had begun to develop a headache from ignoring the premonition that Red was in danger. Vrod regarded him speculatively. 'Brother hurting head again?' There was genuine sympathy in his gravelly voice.

Igorik nodded, knowing that the troll would not attempt to dig into his feelings. That was one of the things he liked about trolls. Vrod's request had been for information and now that he knew why his partner was out of sorts, he felt no need to delve deeper. Vrod peeled away at the first corner, obviously bound for his current favourite haunt, The Purple Wart. Igorik didn't bother warning him to be careful. First, to tell a troll to be careful was a deadly insult because it was tantamount to advising them to be cowards; second, trolls were *always* the instigators of any trouble that happened when they were around. They liked the smell of it, Vrod always told him, leering.

Arriving home twenty minutes later, Igorik dug out his keys and was unlocking his door when he heard a plaintive miaow at his feet. He looked down in disbelief at the little grey cat whose almond-shaped grey eyes glimmered at him expectantly.

'No!' Igorik snarled.

The cat lapped at the milk contentedly, its tail curled daintily around the bowl as if to ensure that Igorik would not remove it before it had been licked scrupulously clean.

'Blasted cat,' Igorik muttered, fingering the small but deep scratch it had left on his forearm the previous day up at the city wall. He couldn't imagine how, let alone why, the wretched thing had followed him all this way down to Lower Quentaris. It was Red that had been patting the damn fleabag. Maybe the idiot thing had somehow got them confused.

His irritation faded as it occurred to him that the cat was the perfect excuse for him to contact Red again. He could send a note demanding that his twin come and collect the animal.

An hour later, Igorik was sitting relaxed in his

wingback armchair with a mug of buttered rum and some pieces of black charcoal that had started out as slices of bread. His decision to contact Red had taken away the pressure of the premonition, but as he ate, he found himself thinking of the woman whose body he had found. He had seen a lot of deaths in the four years since he had become a drainer, but none had affected him like this. It came back to the woman's expression. The hopelessness in it, which reminded him of …

Again his mind tried to drag him back to the past, and again he resisted.

He told himself that he ought to feel pleased because the body salvage had redeemed a week of very slim pickings. Usually the drains were full of stuff that had been abandoned and lost, and which could be sold, or returned for reward. But the fog clogging the streets of Upper Quentaris was keeping people inside and with them, their possessions and purses.

Igorik settled deeper into his chair, relaxing under the combined influence of the warmth of the fire and the buttered rum. The cat had finished its milk and was curled on the hearth by the fire. He ought to get up and put it out, but he was too tired; too comfortable. Besides, maybe the cat deserved an hour by the fire, given that it had provided a means of checking on Red.

His eyes grew heavy.

He fell into a memory dream of searching for Oleg. Quarter elf, half human and quarter of something no one could identify, Oleg was as smart as he was ugly and possessed a wicked gift for mimicry. Igorik hadn't seen him for a few days, and this was unusual enough for him to decide to call at his friend's house. When he had mentioned this intention at breakfast, Red told him casually that he'd better not because he had heard Oleg's mother complaining to a neighbour that her son was sick.

He had gone over to Oleg's house anyway, and had been tersely told that Oleg wasn't home. Another person would have mentioned the rumour that he was sick but Igorik just went away to search in their favourite spots.

In the dream, there was only the last remaining haunt, and it was Igorik's least favourite — a wooden platform built between the two enormously high smoke stacks rising from the outbuildings where potion makers and alchemists brewed up the requirements and ingredients used by magicians. Oleg loved the scents and queer colours that puffed out of the stack to engulf them from time to time, causing brief but sometimes spectacular effects.

The last time they had been there, Oleg had suddenly sprouted long golden hairs from both nostrils. Less funny had been his own ears suddenly growing so immense that they tugged at both sides of his head, giving him an ache that lasted for hours after they had gone back to normal size.

Igorik took a deep breath and began to ascend. As he climbed he found himself thinking about Oleg. Always the one to ask questions, endlessly plaguing Igorik to know what he thought or felt or suspected about this or that, he had lately taken to suddenly falling silent, sometimes in the middle of a joke. He had become morose for long periods of time and had departed abruptly without even saying goodbye. A few times, he had looked at Igorik as if he did not know him. The last time they had been together, Oleg had hinted with twitches and exaggerated grimaces that he knew something important and dangerous. He had kept glancing behind himself as if to surprise someone sneaking up on him.

Igorik squinted up, disliking the way the sun glared down so hotly on his head making spots dance before his eyes. He couldn't see the top of the stack and he fancied there might not be a top, and he would just go on climbing and climbing.

'If there is no top, I won't have to see what is up there,' came the queer and unsettling thought.

'You don't have to go there,' said the low, pleasant voice of a girl.

Igorik almost let go of the rung he was holding onto in shock, for seated on a new platform set lower down the stacks was a slight girl with grey eyes and a long flag of black hair. She was barefoot and swinging her legs back and forwards for all the world as if she were on her own porch instead of perched precariously high above the ground.

'What are you doing here?' Igorik blurted.

'Neither of us is really *here*,' the girl observed. 'You are dreaming of a here-that-was. If you climb higher the dream will become a nightmare.'

Igorik glanced up and had to fight the impulse to go on climbing, despite the growing dread he felt of what awaited him at the top of the stack.

'I can change the dream, if you like,' the girl offered.

Before he could voice his acquiescence, he was standing in a familiar street in Lower Quentaris alongside a food stall he sometimes visited. He was on the verge of taking a seat when he felt someone at his elbow. He glanced sideways, expecting to see Vrod insisting they go to a proper tavern.

Only it wasn't the troll. It was the girl with the long black hair, now clad in grey boots and a supple, dull-golden coat belted at the waist. For some reason the sight of her made him realise that he was no longer a boy.

'Let's see what set off your nightmare, shall we?' She snapped her fingers and Igorik found himself down in the drain tunnels again, kneeling over the drowned woman he had earlier that day pulled from the water. His spirits sank.

'Oh,' said the girl, sounding sick. 'Oh no.'

4

The Dreams of Cats

IGORIK WAS INSIDE ONE of Red's dreams. His twin was gazing up at the roof of the Soothsayers' Guild with such naked longing that Igorik would have groaned if he had any control over himself, but he was never more than an invisible observer in Red's dreams.

'You are linked …' a voice said, but before he could turn to see who had spoken, there was a loud hammering noise and he had the familiar nauseating sensation of being pulled hard by something lodged inside his chest that meant he was waking.

Someone was knocking violently at the door.

He dragged himself out of the chair he had fallen asleep in, noticing with irritation that the grey cat was coiled on the headrest. He waved a hand and it leapt to the floor with an indignant hiss. The banging persisted and Igorik almost stumbled to his knees as he crossed the room. He felt so weak and disoriented that he thought he must be ill.

The moment he had the door open, the cat darted out and away.

'Yours?' Vrod asked.

'No,' Igorik husked. 'I hate cats.'

'Good eating,' Vrod said, glancing after the cat with regret. Then he turned his murky eyes back to Igorik. 'Head bad?'

'I'll be down later,' Igorik told the troll, not having the presence of mind to figure out which bit of him was ailing. 'Better see if you can team with someone else today.'

Vrod paused to digest this news then shrugged pragmatically. 'Vrod not go draining until afternoon. Sister visiting be glad.'

The information that Vrod had a sister who was

visiting was too much on top of the bewildering weakness that was making his legs tremble under him. 'Good,' he managed.

'You want healer?' Vrod demanded.

'No,' Igorik said.

The troll nodded approvingly, having no more regard for healers than for members of the Watch, and departed without further ceremony.

Igorik closed the door and made his way to the kitchen table where there was a dusty mug of water. He drank it thinking one mug of buttered rum and a few slices of burnt toast couldn't have caused such a state, even if the bread *was* a bit mouldy. He crossed to his sink and sluiced what remained of the water in a jug over his head. As he dried, he realised that he wasn't sick so much as strangely weak. Maybe it was the dreams that had filled his sleep and which had left vivid images that would not fade. And the girl! Obviously she represented some part of him, but who would have thought that any bit of his mind would take a form that was so very … female!

She had not only forced him to relive the grim experience of finding the body of the dead woman, she had somehow made him revisit the memories of seeing the two other suicides as well. No one else in the dream memories had seemed to notice her presence and her attention had been entirely focused on the bodies. After that first horrified exclamation, she had not spoken except to point out the similarities between the bodies, some of which he had not noticed, or had not deemed worthy of noting down in his report. It was she who made him see that each body had been dressed in finery of a sort. He had not noticed because of the poverty of the first two bodies, but once she had spoken he had seen it too. The pathetic bit of frayed ribbon around a wrist, a scrap of tinsel knotted in unkempt hair. And of course the body he had found had definitely been dressed for a special occasion. Since when, he wondered, did people dress up to die? Especially given the look of sorrow each of the three had worn. The repetition of that expression of desolation had struck him anew, seeing each of the bodies one after another. Their expressions had not been merely similar, but virtual mirror reflections of one another. As if all had experienced the same impossible sorrow. But even if that could be true, what was the chance of any person's measure of despair being so accurately reflected in another person's face?

It was the girl who pointed out, after somehow

making him replay even depot gossip about the suicides he had not seen, that all of the suicides were alone. 'Suicides generally happen when a person is alone,' Igorik had commented, by this time feeling obscurely that he was being criticised for something. She had given him a cool, measuring look.

'They also *lived* alone which means they could have had company without anyone being aware of it.'

But what could she have meant by that? There had been no evidence to suggest foul play, and the healer who had examined the bodies had noticed nothing untoward. Yet the unnatural similarity in their expressions nagged at him.

The girl had taken them back to the body of the wealthy woman and she had knelt to examine the body with all the delicate efficiency of an investigator. Then she brushed aside the fringe of lank yellow hair to reveal a faint white smudge in the centre of the forehead, virtually invisible on the pale flesh. He had seen her draw back with an expression of revulsion, almost as if that was what she had been searching for.

He might even have asked why she had reacted as she had done, but that was when he had been pulled out of his own dream and into Red's.

Igorik got to his feet with a growl of disgust and changed into fresh drainer gear. He would eat something then go in to the depot and ask a few questions about those bodies while he waited for Vrod, because if nothing else, the dreams had made him realise how uneasy he felt about them.

Katya watched him stride away, thinking that she had been right to focus on this man for without his dreams she would never so swiftly have come upon a trail that might lead her to the Scourge and his minions. Her superior had spoken of the Scourge being responsible for suicides on Astariah, yet he had not detailed the activities that had led to them. Having seen the white marks on the woman's forehead, Katya thought she knew now what those activities might be. One of the signs of Rhianna's tigerish possession of her victims was the leaving of such a mark. It was speculated that it came from physical contact during mind penetration, which allowed a more profound connection. The other bodies found by the drainers had not shown such marks, but Igorik had only seen two, and fleetingly. The problem with delving into a person's memory was that you were limited to what they had seen, consciously or unconsciously. It was the pallor of the bodies that had made her think of a description of Rhianna's victims as ash white, and when she had taken them back to look at the woman Igorik had found, she had been looking for just such a white mark, praying not to find it.

It was suddenly clear to Katya that her superiors were using one abomination to find another. And if both perished in the chase, so much the better. She felt a rush of anger, but regardless of the motives of her superiors, she had agreed to take this mission. The Scourge must be stopped.

She turned her thoughts to Igorik. He was going to need careful handling because his mind was surprisingly perceptive as well as being very wary and private. More than once during the merge, she had felt him look at her suspiciously. One serious mistake and he would perceive her as alien and expel her. Of course she had not intended originally to do more in that first merge than gently introduce herself into his sleeping mind. Drawing him away from his nightmare and seeking the root of it, she had wanted only to present herself as benevolent and nurturing. Then she had seen the body.

Who could have guessed that she would so swiftly

come across evidence of the Scourge's activities? Or that Igorik would be dream-linked to his brother, so that she had been suddenly pulled with Igorik into his twin's dream. The shock of that had awoken her, giving her a dreadful headache which was only now beginning to abate.

Katya sighed. She must begin to search for the Scourge as she had been bidden, but that was going to be complicated by the fact that Igorik had shown no interest in providing the disc that would authorise her to roam Quentaris without fear of capture. She had learned from his dreaming mind why the woman who had smelled of authority at the rift caves had commanded his brother to catch her. At first she had wondered if this new law were not the Scourge's doing, but why would he focus on cats when shape-changers had numerous beast forms? The law was clearly an unfortunate coincidence. Nevertheless, she would have to visit the Archon's palace and see if she could sniff out the Scourge's trail. She had taken plenty of scent samples and she had fixed on the palace as a starting point because on Caris, the Scourge had been guested by the ruler. Her experience was that criminals generally followed the same patterns.

Her orders had been to locate the Scourge and return to Ghast with the information, but having seen the dead woman in the drains, it was clear that her quarry did not mean merely to master rift travelling while he was in Quentaris. He was killing people. First the poor and now it seemed that he had shifted his sights to the upper classes. Since she was under strict instructions not to alert the city to the danger in their midst, she had no choice but to help them protect themselves. She must do something to provoke an investigation that would hamper the Scourge. She would use the dream link between the two brothers to sow the seeds of unease. The Scourge would not give up the advantage he could gain from mastering rift travel merely because local guards were trying to find out who was killing people.

She glanced in the direction that Igorik had gone, hoping that his dreams would already have provoked him enough to make him ask some questions whose answers she could later harvest in dream merge. He smelled of purpose, and though he might merely be consumed by the desire to find better salvage, she doubted it. The suicides had clearly roused unresolved sorrows and confusion about the death of his childhood friend in the big man, and she thought he would not so easily dismiss them.

Katya stiffened, sensing the approach of another feline. It was female and smelled smaller and younger, so she did not assume attack stance but merely arched her back and hissed, laying her ears back. The other cat crept out onto the balcony where she was sitting, a small, skinny black scrap with pale green eyes. It hissed too, but anxiously and with placatory sub notes.

They retained the proper stiffness for a few moments, maintaining eye contact, then Katya relaxed and sat back on her haunches. The other cat miaowed politely and sat too. Katya adjusted her senses for the Quentaran dialect, marvelling that of all animals, cats seemed to be the most ubiquitous in all worlds, and the most kindred. She had never met a cat with whom she could not communicate, but she had met plenty of humans on her own world and on others before the closure of Astariah, that defied understanding.

The she-cat offered its name as Orb and asked Katya if she was intending to remain. It was a territorial question, but politely put. Katya gave her own name, explaining that she was merely visiting a human in the area and did not plan to remain to claim territory. Orb sniffed and said that the human whose dwelling she had come from smelled of troll, and trolls were known cat eaters. Katya avowed that she did not fear trolls because what trolls despised above all was cowardice. If a cat fights they will respect it.

Of course, Katya added, *a troll's respect does not preclude it eating the creature it respects.*

The little cat shivered and gave her an admiring glance.

This gave Katya an idea. She asked if Orb's territory extended at any point into Upper Quentaris. It took some effort to explain what she meant, for it transpired that Orb had been born in Lower Quentaris, and seemed hardly to believe there were such things as a moon and stars, let alone another level of the city. At length, she told Katya that she had never been to Upper Quentaris, but that she could ask those whose territories bordered her own.

'What seeks Katya?' she asked curiously. 'Mate-scent?'

Katya would have burst out laughing had she been in human form, for she had never encountered anyone whose scent had snared her heart and soul.

'I will show what Katya seeks,' she miaowed, and moved to sit beside the cat. She pressed her paw to the other cat's face and tentatively entered the waking dream that was the cat's mind. After an initial start of surprise, Orb watched Katya reshape dream matter to form a hazy human image from which emanated a collection of unpleasant and slightly alarming notes and olfactory sub notes. The cat hissed softly that the smell seemed repugnant and dangerous to her. 'Why does Katya-cat-dreamer seek human-that-smells-of-wrongness?'

Katya could not think how to explain so she produced an image of Orb, coming to the window of Igorik's hovel that night and receiving more scraps. The chance of the small stray finding her quarry was slender, of course. Nevertheless she might be lucky. Luck, good or bad, was often a significant factor in an investigation.

Orb departed, leaving Katya to sit washing her ears until her energy was fully restored. She had no idea why she could enter the mind of a cat so easily, but not other beasts. There was no book she could consult aside from the tomes dealing with Rhianna, and even in these very little was said about the powers the shape-changer had possessed. Katya had always suspected the details had been deliberately censored to ensure no one else could learn her secrets.

But it seemed that at least one other had done so …

She set off to find the Archon's palace, summoning to mind all she had been told of Quentaris. The city was not ruled from afar nor was it the ruling city of its planet. It was an autonomous city state, and like the other near city states of Hadran, Simesian, Tolrush and Brunt, had its own ruler. In the past, so Ghast historians had written, there had been kings and queens of Quentaris, as well as other forms of government, but at present there was the Archon. His palace was reputed to be enormous, housing the mechanism of government in a multitude of offices, as well as ceremonial rooms and halls. There were also lavish apartments occupied by the Archon, his large entourage, and numerous officials and members of the court. Close by were the Halls of Justice, described by one Ghastian trader as a long, low and forbidding series of buildings comprising the courts for Quentaris, the headquarters of the City Watch and the dungeons in which prisoners awaiting justice, or having had justice dispensed, were housed.

It was near dusk by the time Katya decided to head back to Lower Quentaris. Since she was quite close to the cliffs that contained the magical tangle of portals Quentarans called rifts, she decided to use the same route as when she had tailed Igorik. During the day she had smelled a number of entries to the under city, but all had been choked with rubble or had smelled of small malevolencies.

She had not managed to find any trace of the Scourge about the Archon's palace, but then again she had been unable to do a truly thorough search for fear of being caught by some official or citizen who would hand her over to the stray cat squad.

Giving up on the Archon's palace for the moment, she had been sitting on a rim of guttering deciding what to do next when two men had struck up a conversation in the street below. To her delight one announced his intention to visit the orientation centre where guides went to meet with those who wished to use their services. She had followed, but there had been no chance of tracking a guide because she did not know how to tell which of the few people she saw entering were guides. A day of observation and eavesdropping would correct that, but she could just as easily find out if there were some means of identifying them from Igorik. She must also try to find a way to make him purchase the red disc that would mark her as an owned cat, because then she could search properly for the Scourge's trail.

Passing along the top of the rift wall, she was interested to see that at this end of the cliffs, there were much bigger caves than the one she had come through, and not all were accessible at ground level. One was large enough to admit a laden cart pulled by a team of bullocks and Katya wondered how high the cliffs went. It was impossible to see because of the fog and again she wondered if it was a permanent fixture in Quentaris. She was beginning to long for a wide vista, or a glimpse of the stars or sunlight.

She heard a step and flattened against the top of the wall, certain she would not be seen if she remained still, a grey cat against a grey wall. But as the human came close and passed through a small gate in the rift wall, locking it behind him, she was startled to realise that it was Igorik's twin brother.

His scent was unmistakable. Her human senses dismissed this near encounter as a coincidence, but her cat senses insisted with a frisson of excitement that it was no coincidence. As he passed along the lane leading back to the street that ran parallel to the rift wall, she turned tail and followed him.

5

A Strange Sea

RED WAS DEPRESSED AND his head ached. The day had dragged because, aside from enduring two back-to-back punishment shifts for slacking and letting the cat escape, he had been stupefyingly bored. Hardly anyone in the city was bothering to use the rifts. Not even regular trade shipments had gone out today. The only traffic had been the other way and he could count them on one hand: one guided expedition returning from some months away, a couple of girls who had been fossil hunting in a cave on their world and had ended up in Quentaris by chance, and a group of sentient snakes seeking a potion for scale rot.

Not that he desired excitement. What he most wanted was to go to his bed and lie down. But if he did, he feared that Iakas would slip from his mind again. He had to see her and try to explain, though what he could say, he still did not know. All day part of him had said it was pointless even to bother trying. She would be angry and she would not listen. But a stubborn bit of him kept thinking of how she looked when she was excited, or when she flung her head back and laughed. Or how the grace of her movements over the roofs delighted his senses. These images had enabled him to fight the weight of the lethargy that dragged at him like a sodden cloak.

He stopped at the steps leading up to the ornate doors of the Soothsayers' Guild. He could see neither the roof nor any sign of her roost atop it because of the cursed fog and again it seemed to him that he was foolish in coming here. Of course she would not believe he had forgotten through no fault of his own.

But then the memory of Iakas's smile lit his heart

and he shook his head. He would not give her up without a fight, even if she were the one fighting him. He began to climb up the wall from one jutting bit of stonework to the next. He could have gone inside and used the steps. The soothsayers had never shown the slightest sign of resenting roofies in general and Iakas in particular. But Red always got the feeling that she secretly despised those who asked permission and used doors and stairs.

He was shocked when, after climbing for some minutes, his head suddenly rose *above* the level of the fog. It was as if he had broken through the surface of a pond of grey soup which gave off coils and tendrils of steam.

Being able to see suddenly so far in all directions made him dizzy and he tightened his grip and sucked in a few deep steadying breaths of fresh sweet air, only now realising that the fog had a stale non-smell; like old crumbly biscuits left in a jar too long. Gradually the dizziness faded, leaving a welling elation that nevertheless felt as if it were struggling up from his boots. He gazed around thinking that from this point of view, it really looked as if a gelid grey sea had drowned the city and was now lapping sluggishly at the soaring cliffs which rose ten times higher above the fog than the Soothsayers' Guild house.

Visitors from beyond the rifts often described the cliffs as 'looming' over Quentaris, but to him their presence had always been reassuring. For some minutes he simply drank in the sight of their familiar jagged edge soaring above. But as his eyes adjusted to the radiance of full daylight for the first time in weeks, he looked around and saw that other buildings also pierced the fog; the Cathedral of the Holy Benefactor Mushin, Pandro's Tower. The Soothsayers' tower rose higher than them all.

Red began to climb again. By the time he had reached the roof, he had all but forgotten the view in his anxiety. He saw at once from the open flap of her roost that Iakas was inside, and he deliberately scuffed a shingle. She emerged swiftly, smiling welcome, but the momentary brightness in her face dimmed instantly when she saw who her visitor was.

'Iakas,' he began, wondering with a stab of jealousy who that smile had been for.

'What are you doing here?' she asked.

His heart plummeted at the flat tone of her voice. Seeing her he had experienced such a surge of longing that he had nearly reached out for her. He stammered stupidly, 'I … I missed your name-day celebration.'

'Yes,' she said coldly. 'Well, it wasn't important.'

Oh, how Red longed for his old careless sense of humour that would have given him the right words to melt her, but caring so much seemed to have drained him of all wit and laughter. He found he could only say exactly what he felt. 'It *was* important! I truly don't know how I missed it. I was so happy when you asked me.' He broke off because he had been about to say that he wanted to be alone with her, but just in time realised this had been *his* interpretation of her invitation.

'Yet you forgot,' Iakas pointed out.

'I didn't!' he said, and she lifted a winged brow. 'All right I did, but I don't know how I could have done.'

He sounded so honestly confounded that inwardly Iakas softened. But the humiliating memory of sitting alone on the roof with her special supper for two, the candles gradually burning away to nothing, was too keen for her to easily bend.

'All I know is that it seems like there is an epidemic of forgetfulness and apathy in Quentaris these days,' she said stiffly. 'Not long ago there was all this talk about roofies being awarded squatter status. But I can't get sense out of anyone at the Archon's palace or the Halls of Justice. I can't even get an advocate to represent us. And the other roofies don't care. It's my fault, of course. I'm not inspiring enough to hold them together.'

She looked so dejected that Red had a renewed desire to take her in his arms and kiss the trouble out of her woebegone little face. But he only said, 'Of course you are inspiring to them. There must be some other reason for them being the way they are.'

'What reason?' Iakas demanded, not giving an inch.

'It … it could be something in the air,' Red said wildly. 'The fog …'

'Oh, and how is it that I have not been affected by it then?'

Red thought that nothing as vague as fog would ever stand a chance with someone whose mind was so bright and focused. But he said, 'You … you live above the fog line.'

'I was down in the streets all yesterday at the Archon's palace trying to make the Watch assigned to the gate let me in. I swear they seemed half-witted.'

'Maybe … maybe the fog only affects you when you're in it constantly. I mean, I visited Igorik in

Lower Quentaris and woke up the next day feeling fine, but after yesterday and today on duty I can hardly think straight.' Even as he uttered the words, he felt the truth of them. 'That might even be why the other roofies are apathetic. Yours is the only roost on a roof above the fog line.'

Iakas looked around, and letting his own eyes track her gaze, Red found himself wondering if the fog really could be affecting people. Didn't he feel more clear-headed and alert now out of the fog, than he had done all day down in it fulfilling his punishment duty? This thought reminded him that he had neglected to report completion of punishment duty. In Cora's present mood that would earn him another double shift. Then he wondered if it might not be the fog that was making Cora so moody and introverted.

He rose and Iakas looked up at him; the sun was on the point of setting behind her, turning her into a shadow. 'I ought to go and …'

'Fine,' she said.

Red hesitated, but the dismissal in her tone gave him nowhere to go. 'All right,' he said.

Why didn't he just kiss her? Katya wondered, watching the man depart. From her vantage point beside a chimney pot, she growled in her throat at the stupidity of humans. They lacked the simple but vital animal ability to scent the yearning at the heart of all their haze of words.

The young woman now stood gazing at the point on the roof where the man had vanished, smelling of tears.

Katya padded away.

Igorik stomped to the door, opened it and looked down wrathfully. The grey cat blinked mildly up at him and a bit of him was unwillingly impressed with its persistence. He opened his mouth to shout at it to go away and then he remembered the note he had sent to Red. His feeling that his twin was in danger had faded since he had sent it, but that might only be the effect of his acting on the premonition. In any case, he had better have the cat he had commanded Red to come and fetch. He stepped back and it stretched in a leisurely fashion before entering. It went straight to the hearth to inspect the fire, then turned as if to ask where its supper was.

'Unbelievable!' Igorik muttered, but he poured milk into a bowl and set it down. The cat arched against his hand before he could snatch it away and he was startled at the softness of its fur. He felt a jab of guilt at his intention to betray the little animal to Red.

'The air will probably be better outside the city,' he muttered. 'And you can always sneak back in.'

The cat paid no attention to him. Its ferocious absorption in the milk reminded him of Vrod's single-mindedness when he worked. Which made the troll's decision to take a morning off rather than seek another partner all the more striking. It told Igorik what he had known for some time without acknowledging it. The troll liked him. Ironic given that he had only accepted a partner because Vrod was a troll and trolls were supposed to be incapable of friendship with their own kind let alone humans. But it seemed friendship could sneak up and ambush you from behind when you were least expecting it.

He was too tired to decide what he felt about this. The crack of the dying fire and the soft regular lapping sound the cat made as it drank were hypnotic and after nodding off several times, he decided he might as well lie down. If Red came, he had his own key. They could talk in the morning.

His last conscious thought was an order to himself not to dream.

In the dream, Igorik was a boy again, swimming in a small deep lake formed between several great jutting slabs of white stone at one end of a disused quarry. The water had a cloudy aqua hue, but where sunlight shafted down through the fringe of trees showing above the stone it fractured into ripples and feathery strands of green radiance. Igorik swam slowly, enjoying the rare lightness that water lent his movements.

He glanced back and was horrified to see that there was nothing on the high flat rock where he traditionally left his clothes. He struck out for the rock with mortifying visions of having to creep naked back into the city, but when he hauled himself out of the water, he was startled to find both his clothes and the dark-haired girl of his dreams on the rock. With a yelp of alarm, he dropped back into the water, waiting until he had to before resurfacing, and hoping she would take his redness as the result of too much sun.

'You do have a great nostalgia for your boyhood, don't you?' she murmured, a touch of amusement in her husky voice. But her eyes were serious and their gravity touched some buried apprehension in him.

'I … I … What do you want?'

Her eyes widened and he realised as he had not done before, that there was a cloud of gold in the centre of her eyes. Was it really possible that a bit of his mind had taken the shape of a female non-human? It seemed impossible.

'What do *I* want?' she echoed, reminding him of his question. 'The question ought to be, what do *you* want?'

Igorik grew angry. 'I want to get dressed!' He hoped she would take the hint and go away. Instead, she lifted a hand and suddenly he was sitting on the rock next to her, fully dressed.

She said, 'You went to see your superior today about the suicides.'

He felt a shock at her knowledge of his activities, then realised that of course his mind knew what he had been doing. Then he found himself reliving his interview earlier that day with the blond and monosyllabic chief of the salvage depot, only in reality there had been no mysterious girl at his side clad in grey boots and a golden coat and listening intently as Igorik pointed out the similarity between the suicides. Arick waited until he was finished with that slightly annoying, meticulous courtesy of his, and then pointed out that he had made a report to the Archon's office of statistics on the increase in suicides. He looked down at his desk and Igorik took this as a dismissal, but as he was turning to the door, Arick lifted his head to say that one of the secretaries in the Archon's palace who had just come back from a holiday in Tolrush had mentioned that there had been a noticeable increase in suicides in Upper Quentaris.

'Upper Quentaris,' Arick said pointedly, the implication being that this made it a matter for the City Watch.

'You must find out if these suicides fit the profile of the bodies we have already seen,' the girl urged when they were outside the depot.

'No official will answer the questions of a lowly drainer,' Igorik growled, wondering how a bit of his own mind could formulate sentences with words he didn't even know. But he was distracted to find himself back by the quarry pool sitting on the same rock, only now it was night and the girl's eyes seemed faintly luminous.

'If those who are official will not give you information, then find someone unofficial who will,' she said. Her tone was less imperious than before, but Igorik got the feeling she was suppressing impatience. Again he was tempted to ask what right a bit of his own mind had to interrogate him and make him feel inadequate. But then he realised there *was* someone unofficial he could ask. Ma Coglin! There was little that went on in Quentaris that the immense mistress of the Paupers' Market did not know, according to Red. She was the terror of upper-class Quentaran kitchens, badgering and bullying them endlessly into donations of food which she would then dole out in scrupulous fairness to the needy, most of whom she knew by name.

'Do *you* have a name?' Igorik asked the girl suddenly.

She looked wary. 'My name is Katya.'

'Katya is …' Igorik had been about to say very female, but instead he said gruffly, 'fine.'

She shrugged. 'Maybe you could suggest to

whomever you talk to, that it is not safe for people to go about alone, nor to open their doors to strangers, no matter how respectable they seem.'

Igorik stared at her, his unease growing, though he could not have said why. It centred on this girl though. This figment of his imagination who knew what he had done and heard his thoughts, but who seemed to be outside his will.

'You told your troll friend?' Katya asked softly.

Again Igorik was diverted, this time by the girl calling Vrod a friend, as much as by her knowing what he had been doing. He said, 'I talked to Vrod about the suicides. He didn't say anything but that doesn't mean he won't nose around. People think trolls are dull-witted because they are so big and they move slowly and talk and think slowly. But slowness doesn't mean they are stupid. He might not ask, though, because the bodies are human and trolls don't get involved with humans.'

'*You* are human,' Katya said softly. 'He cares for you.'

Igorik glanced down at the rippling moonlit surface of the quarry pool and felt an unaccountable surge of sorrow. 'Look, I just don't see the point of all this. I mean, I know the suicides are bothering me. You are the proof of that. But even if there is some reason people are committing suicide it's not like we can stop them.'

'*If* they are suicides,' Katya said.

'What are you trying to suggest? It can't be murder because not a single Watch captain or healer has found cause to wonder at the verdict of suicide. And what motive would there be anyway? There is no gain since most of the dead are poor.'

Katya was frowning and he had the distinct feeling she was trying to decide something. At last she said softly, persuasively, 'What if the murders were being committed in some way that no one would recognise, for some reward that you could not imagine?'

'A murderer from one of the worlds beyond the rifts?' Igorik muttered. Katya was watching him closely. Waiting, he thought.

At length she said, 'Perhaps there is a list of those who come through the rifts.'

'Of course,' Igorik said, wondering how one minute she could know everything in his mind and the next, seem ignorant of the simplest thing. 'There is a ledger at the palace which the Watch compiles, but I wouldn't be allowed to just march up and look at it. I'd have to apply.'

'Your brother could manage it without permission,' she said.

'That is a good idea, but we should try to pinpoint the first related suicide before I ask him.' Then he frowned. 'Wait a minute, I don't know how it is in Upper Quentaris, but I *know* when the first suicide was found in the drains. It was right after that fog came in, because the other drainers were talking about it when the body was brought in.'

He stopped because Katya was staring at him out of suddenly enormous eyes. 'What is it?

'The fog,' she whispered.

'What about it?' Igorik demanded. She did not answer. 'Are you saying the fog might have something to do with the suicides?'

'I do not know,' Katya said. 'But perhaps for the sake of Quentaris, I had better find out.'

Suddenly she vanished, and Igorik was left staring at the moonlit rock where she had been sitting.

6

Of Shadow-Which-Bleeds

ATYA PUSHED THROUGH THE half-opened shutter and found Orb waiting expectantly on the sill. She had managed to find a bit of larded bread on the table and hoped this would be acceptable. She need not have worried, for Orb fell on the scrap with famished attention, growling in the back of her throat as she ate.

Katya watched, her human aspect full of pity. How was it that in all worlds so many small ones went hungry while others gorged? Was it never possible for the inhabitants of worlds to understand that they were part of a body greater than one life, all of which must be nourished for that greater body to remain healthy?

Having dispatched her meagre supper, Orb began preening herself industriously. Katya groomed her own tail to keep the small animal company, then, the niceties preserved, asked what she had learned. Orb said regretfully that no cat had recognised the scent of the human that Katya sought, but the cats questioned would enquire of cats at the outer edges of their own territories. Tomorrow, Orb would bring another report.

Katya thanked her and then something prompted her to ask, 'Did any cat speak of that-which-blinds-the-air?'

Orb considered the question. 'Some from the overcity told of shadow-which-bleeds but Orb does not know if it is that-which-blinds-the-air.'

'What do they say of shadow-which-bleeds? Do they say where it bleeds from?'

'One says from the humans,' Orb surprisingly said.

'But it affects them …' Katya murmured to herself.

'Other cats say shadow-which-bleeds makes humans stupid and blind and deaf and that it has eaten the sun, yet hungers still.'

'For what does it hunger?' Katya asked.

'For light, some say. For laughter, say others. For life, said one.'

'Does shadow-that-bleeds make animals or birds dull and stupid?' Orb said it did not seem so. 'Why did one cat believe shadow-that-bleeds comes from humans?' Katya asked.

'He saw it bleeding from the body of mistress-who-died.'

Katya's human aspect churned with speculations, but her cat-self quelled them. She asked calmly, 'Could you bring cat of mistress-who-died here? There would be food for him also.'

'I will bring him,' Orb promised.

After she had gone, Katya thought about the fog. She had no doubt the Scourge was behind it. It would be too much of a coincidence for a fog inducing passivity and dullness to enshroud Quentaris at the very moment he and his minions were killing its citizens. He must have discovered some artefact or power during his long years on Caris, and was using it to subdue the city. She was certain that she had even read something on Caris about a persistent fog that had settled over one city. Yet what did it mean that a cat claimed to have seen it coming from his dying mistress? Could the cat be mistaken? Unless the fog was what had killed the supposed suicides? Katya grew excited at the thought that the mistress of the cat that Orb would bring might be one of the so-called suicides.

Katya turned her thoughts back to the Scourge and wondered for the first time *why* he killed people. Rhianna had possessed her victims in order to use them to do her will. Those that had died had done so only in the doing of her will. So what was the Scourge doing? The only thing Katya could think was that it had something to do with what her superior had called *unnatural appetites*. At the time she had taken his words as meaning the Scourge's appetite for power, but now she wondered if there was not some actual appetite being fed.

Orb, too, had spoken of the fog as hungering.

She sang a little of her puzzlement to the invisible moon, as cats do, and her mind grew calm. As with other cases, she lacked some vital piece of information needed to solve the puzzle. If only she knew what the Scourge had done to cause the deaths of his fellow students before fleeing Astariah, she might understand what was happening in Quentaris. She could return to Ghast and demand more information from her superior. But until she learned how to negotiate the rifts she was trapped on this world.

That must be her next priority, she decided. She would find a guide before the night was out, track him or her down and dream merge to find out how to use the rift which would bring her back to Ghast. Guides wore no specific uniforms, but there were mannerisms and habits and fads in attire that she had learned from Igorik's mind, that would aid her in identifying one.

She rose and arched her back, twitching her tail with impatience.

Igorik had awakened again that morning with an aching head, a weakness in his limbs that had taken a good hour to wear off, and more dream memories centred around the girl his mind had conjured up. Instead of giving in to the malaise, he forced himself to rise, dress and meet Vrod as usual. They spent the day in the drains, though with little result. Partly it was scarcity of salvage and partly it was his inability to concentrate. Twice he had managed to miss snagging things, one a bag which had looked rich enough to contain a purse. He was glad Vrod had been working another part of the drain at that point.

By the time the day was over, he had no thought but to visit Red. He wanted to find out why his twin had not responded to his message, and also to ask him to look at the arrivals ledger. Because Katya, as that animated bit of his mind had strangely named itself, was right in suggesting that a murderer who had come through the rift *might* be killing in some unrecognisable way. If he could just make someone in authority see how impossibly similar the suicides were, they might at least check on the recent arrivals. He had already decided not to bother going to Arick. The salvage depot manager would simply file a report. Igorik would go to the Archon's palace and make someone listen to what he had to say.

He had bidden Vrod a distracted farewell and hastened home to change. There had been no sign of the cat and he was irritated to find himself worrying if the cat squad had picked it up. Idiotic when the wretched thing had probably already crept back into the city by now. Dismissing it from his thoughts, he washed and dressed swiftly, knowing he could not appear before officials stinking of the drains. For the same reason, he took a more distant exit route from Lower Quentaris. His usual route would have got him filthy. He arrived in Upper Quentaris not far from the palace, but he turned back towards the rift caves automatically, because the premonition that Red was in danger had suddenly grown more insistent.

He had almost passed a small lane entrance when he noticed a sign pointing into it said Paupers' Market. Telling himself it would not take long, he shifted his coin pouch to the front of his belt and entered the narrow lane.

'Well now, what have we here?' Ma Coglin asked in her booming voice.

Igorik was relieved that the bare grey paupers' kitchen was all but deserted. 'You won't remember me, ma'am,' he began gruffly.

She cut him off with a loud laugh. 'I remember you, lad. The silent one of a matched pair.' He was genuinely startled. She grinned. 'Your brother comes here from time to time to give us a hand and for all your likeness, I can see you are not him.' Her eyes narrowed and she studied him momentarily in silence, then she said, 'Maybe you should think of giving some time here, too. It is almost miraculous how sorrow vanishes in the face of greater sorrows. Not that we have so many customers since this curst fog.' She glanced out through the open sides of the kitchen at the coiling grey mist which seemed thicker than ever today. He wanted to speak but was unsettled by her mention of sorrow. What did she mean?

Ma Coglin goggled at him. 'Well your silences are weighty, but you will have to put them into words for me to judge if they are also meaningful.' She laughed and the laughter sounded too loud in all that emptiness and silence. She saw him flinch and sighed. 'Bad times when laughter becomes an unwelcome stranger.'

'I wanted to ask about suicides,' Igorik said, unable to think of any elegant way to introduce what he wanted to say.

Her gaze seemed to sharpen. Investigator's eyes, he thought. His father's description for eyes that missed nothing. 'Funny you should mention suicides,' she said. 'Four people who used to come here have killed themselves in the last few weeks. Might explain why so few have been making use of us lately. Maybe people are beginning to feel this is an unlucky place.'

'I don't believe in luck,' Igorik said and, heartened by her bluntness, he told her about the suicides that had washed up in the drain, pointing out the similarities between them. She began nodding. It transpired that she had been called in to identify all of those suicides in Upper Quentaris, who were clearly flotsam.

'They all had that look you're describing, lad. Like everything they loved was dead and gone. Fair made my heart sink. Funny thing is, I wouldn't have said any of them were so low at heart, for all they were flotsam. Rich folk and nobility always imagine no one can be happy without what they have, but it's not so. An urchin who finds a whole hot pie can feel ecstasy and I'd say his ecstasy is all the keener for the lacks in his life.'

Igorik asked her to describe the bodies she had seen, stopping her when she mentioned a white mark on the cheek of one. 'Like a frozen kiss mark,' she elaborated. Then she angled a ferocious glare that made him step back a pace. 'Are you saying they were not suicides?'

Igorik realised her ire was not directed at him. 'I don't believe they killed themselves any more than the ones who died in the drains did. There are too many of them and too many similarities. I think someone or something came through a rift and is killing them in some way the healers don't recognise.'

Ma Coglin nodded. 'My thoughts have been riding the same way, lad. Though I thought someone might have come through carrying a plague of despair that they were spreading. Maybe without even knowing it.'

It was a good idea and he would mention it to Katya, Igorik thought. Then he felt a lurch of unease because for a second, he had been thinking about her as if she was real, rather than just a dream persona. A fine time to start going off his head, he chided himself.

Ma Coglin went on, 'I guess you will ask me next if I have heard any gossip that might lead you to the murderer, but what little gossip I hear these days is all about how half the city can't get out of bed to feed itself. Stalls don't open, hospitals have no healers. I think it's the fog. Filthy stuff. I'm glad I live in Lower Quentaris. For a while I thought it might be the fog causing people to suicide.' She fixed him with a penetrating look. 'So, what will you do?'

He told her, thinking half-distractedly of what she had said about the fog. Katya had mentioned the fog too.

'Not much of a plan,' Ma Coglin said sourly. 'But I don't see how you could come up with better, knowing so little. One thing, though. Maybe instead of worrying about official ledgers, you can just ask that brother of yours. He was on ledger duty around the time I was called to identify poor little Flossie who was the first suicide, and so he would have spoken to every arrival around then to get their signature or mark. Maybe he'll remember something.'

'I'll ask him. I was going to see him before I went to the palace.'

'He will not be on duty. I saw him pass this morning heading away from the cliffs and he was not in uniform.'

'Blast,' Igorik muttered, remembering his note. No doubt Red had gone to see him. He would probably wait at Igorik's house. Igorik shrugged. Having heard what Ma Coglin said, he was more anxious to speak to someone official. Somewhere out there in the befogged city was a murderer looking for another victim.

'Maybe he is visiting that pretty roofie he's so keen on,' Ma Coglin said, with a flash of mischief.

It ought to have been macabre for her to talk in such a way at such a moment, but there was something irrepressible about the old woman that lifted Igorik's spirits. No wonder Red went to help out at the Paupers' Market. He might just do the same once this was all over. But now, he would go to the palace, and maybe since it was on the way, he would call into the Soothsayers' Guild and see if Red was there.

He was about to take his leave when Ma Coglin caught his arm in a surprisingly powerful grip.

'You let me know what you find out, lad.'

'I'll send an urchin,' he promised, 'but one thing you can do is tell anyone who comes here not to sleep alone or go about the streets alone. Nor accept any offers from strangers. Tell them there is a killer in the city murdering in some new invisible way and they are targeting loners.'

'Officials would order me to say nothing in case of panic,' Ma Coglin said. 'Panic is bad for business.'

'I don't care about business,' Igorik said.

Ma Coglin clapped his back so hard his teeth rattled. 'You are made of good stuff, lad. Solid, reliable material that doesn't break easily.'

Igorik walked swiftly along the lane wondering if this was what his father had felt. This compelling sense of being on the trail of something vital. This ferocious determination to right a wrong. He had always imagined investigating was nothing but rules, poking your nose into other people's business and dealing with paperwork. He had wondered why his father did it when it so distressed his mother.

For the first time, he felt that he almost understood the passion for investigation that had killed his father.

Iakas was astonished to find the great wrought-iron doors to the guides' orientation centre shut. Everyone knew that the place stayed open day and night because of rift travellers constantly arriving and wanting to register themselves or to be given aid, or merely to get directions. Then there were always people wanting to travel somewhere difficult who had to book a guide.

Was it possible she had called just when they were having some sort of important meeting? She sighed and sat on a stone bench. She would wait until someone else came along to ask.

Inevitably her thoughts swung to Red.

The invitation to her name-day feast had been the last of a lovely period of frequent visits. When the handsome rift guard had not come again and had failed to come on her name-day night, she thought that he had lost interest in her. She had managed to convince herself it didn't matter until she had come out of her roost the previous dusk to find him smiling at her. All logic had been swept away by the delight that had risen unstoppably at the sight of him. Of course she had clamped down on that traitorous joy at once. But then he had spoken and although his explanations and stumbling excuses had been pathetic, her heart had insisted on her believing that he really didn't know why he had forgotten. The look in his eyes had been his best argument, for it mirrored her own longing. Yet the hurt of those days when he had not come and had sent no note, and the pain of that lonely name-day evening, had made her stiff.

He ought to have stayed longer, she thought with ire. Given her a chance to thaw. Instead he had gone suddenly and abruptly. But after she had got over feeling upset and abandoned, she had found herself remembering what he had said about the fog, and had become convinced that he was right. The fog *was* affecting people's minds. She had only to think of the roofies she had visited; the way they sat listless and lank-haired, their eyes dull and their roosts filthy. The more she thought, the more alarmed she had grown. Finally, she had realised that she must act. She had made a few strategic preparations before spending the entire night running over the roofs of Quentaris visiting one roofie after another, insisting they all attend a meeting at her roost at midday the next day. It was almost that time now and she hoped that the roofies she had managed to rouse were there, eating the food she had left, sipping mead, arguing and breathing clean air. She had left a note asking them to wait, claiming to have been summoned to an emergency meeting with the Archon. Absurd, but she had been in too much of a hurry to think of a better excuse for her absence.

She trusted the fog-dulled wits of the roofies to accept her note and calculated that if she went back at dusk, they would be restored enough to listen to what she wanted to say.

In the meantime, she had made up her mind to go and tell the guides what she believed. After the last few days, she had no faith in the Archon's office. She had wanted to ask Red to come with her, given that he was friends with the renowned guide, Rad de La'rel, but had been unable to find him on or off duty. One of the watchmen at the rifts, dull-eyed as any of the roofies, mumbled that Red had probably gone to Lower Quentaris to see his brother.

Iakas sighed in vexation at the memory. She got up and mounted the stone steps to the enormous iron doors. Surely they should not be closed, even if there was a meeting. She lay a hand on the cold metal, wondering suddenly if it were closed because all of the guides had fallen into the same state as the roofies. After all they had been breathing in the fog just like everyone else living in Quentaris.

She turned and squinted at the vague outlines of houses and buildings with the sudden chilling thought that all over Quentaris, people were sitting dull and mindless, starving or needing water, but without the will to fetch it. Soon, perhaps, people would begin to die.

She turned to the doors and hammered at them in a mingled surge of fear and frustration. The loud gonging that resulted made her heart race, and she stepped back. It was so quiet and the streets were so empty. It was as if she were the last person alive in all Quentaris.

And how long before the fog would begin to erode *her* will?

She heard the door open and turned in relief to find an older guide with a long white beard looking out at her. His eyes were unfocused and his expression vague, but he must have had some wit left if he had come to open the door.

But then she saw a woman step into the gap behind him. A tall beautiful woman with pale eyes and a glittering green dress. The faint spiralling cloud of emerald at the centre of her eyes revealed her to be a rift traveller and exactly matched the hue of a glittering and jewel-studded torc about her white neck.

'Why are the doors closed?' Iakas asked, wondering if the woman's eyes were clear and alert simply because she had recently come through a rift, or because the fog did not affect her.

The woman's dark brows lifted. 'I am Rolynna, child. I am afraid I do not know why the doors are closed. I am a member of a trade delegation being guested in Quentaris. Perhaps you should come in and speak to someone who can help you.' She set her hand on the old man's shoulder and as he shuffled aside, he seemed to pale before her eyes.

Iakas looked back at the woman and caught a furtive gleam in those strange eyes. Before she could think what it might mean, the old guide stumbled to his knees.

Iakas hurried to help him up. 'What is the matter?'

'He is ill,' Rolynna said in a soothing voice, pulling him upright. 'Perhaps you will help me get him back to his chair.'

Iakas took one of the old man's arms over her shoulders and the woman took the other, offering a brilliant smile as she pushed the door closed behind them.

7

The Scourge

ATYA RETURNED TO IGORIK'S house and this time he opened the door as soon as she scratched at it. She saw at once that he was too preoccupied to be annoyed. When he got her a bowl of milk without her having to ask for it, she began to feel apprehensive. But all she could make of his mutters was that he was again experiencing premonitions about his brother.

She waited impatiently for him to become tired, but Igorik was too agitated, and paced restlessly for an hour before he lay down. Even then he tossed and turned for another hour before falling asleep.

Katya forced herself to wait until he had descended into a level of sleep deep enough that he would not easily wake. Then she leapt onto his bed and settled herself delicately under his chin. It would have worked just as well to rest against the back of his head, but she rather liked the warmth and male scent of the gliding curve from his chest to his chin.

She let her mind slip into his and found that he was dreaming about looking for something in what she guessed were the under caverns of Quentaris. She felt the current of anxiety running through the dream tug at her and had to fight not to start searching frantically, too. Katya knew she must get his attention in order to slow the mindless current. She called his name several times, but he did not hear her. She tried again, also willing him fiercely to notice her and at last, to her immense relief, he looked at her.

'What do you want? I am busy,' he demanded curtly.

The cat in her wanted to hiss at him, but she merely asked what he was looking for. The question seemed to trouble the big drainer and his eyes skated around vaguely. Katya said quickly, 'Igorik, you are worried about your brother. Tell me why.'

For a moment she feared the anxiety driving the dream was too strong, but at length he began to describe the powerful premonition that his twin was in deadly danger which had struck him just as he was leaving the Soothsayers' tower. He had intended to go to the Archon's palace next, but the premonition had hammered into him, shattering his resolve and had sent him back down to Lower Quentaris looking for his twin. Red had not been in his house so Igorik had made up his mind there was no point in searching until morning. He was finding the wait difficult to endure.

'I have to find him,' Igorik muttered for the fifth time. His eyes shifted to the caverns which were suddenly growing and multiplying in complexity.

'Maybe he is with Iakas.' Even as she spoke, Katya heard in the soft mind babble running through the dream that Iakas had been absent when Igorik had gone up to her roost, though almost every other roofie had been there apparently having been invited by her.

Katya guessed that the roofie girl had taken to heart Red's suggestion that the fog was dangerous, and had deliberately lured the other roofies high enough to get them out of it. No doubt her absence was deliberate, to give them time to recover their wits. She might even have gone to see Red, and they were waiting out the night somewhere together. If so, they must have gone up high, because if they had taken refuge in the under city, they would certainly have come to Igorik.

When she suggested all of this to the big drainer, he shook his head. 'Ma Coglin saw Red this morning and he was alone. Anyway if Red and Iakas were together, why would I be having premonitions of danger?'

Katya managed in time to avoid saying that they could *both* be in danger. Then she registered the soft babble that offered her glimpses of Igorik's conversation with Ma Coglin.

'She saw a white mark on one of the bodies,' she murmured, wishing she dared demand that Igorik replay the conversation with the older woman. But her presence in the dream was too unstable to risk pushing him.

Igorik said, 'Ma Coglin suggested that if I wanted

to find out who has come through the rifts lately, I ought to talk to Red. He was in charge of the ledgers so he would have seen everyone or thing who came through.'

Katya's heart quickened. If Igorik was right, she could simply dream merge with Red and scroll through his memories until she saw the Scourge and his minions. But where was Red?

To her surprise, Igorik answered as if she had spoken aloud. 'I thought he might have gone to see Rad, so before I came to down Lower Quentaris, I went to his house. Rad's girlfriend, Tulcia, was there. I managed to rouse her enough for her to tell me that Rad was just back from an expedition, but a messenger had come from the palace to get him.'

Katya's skin prickled. 'Rad is a guide?'

'The best,' Igorik said. 'Why?'

Katya could not tell him without telling him everything, so she changed the subject. 'You know, maybe you could *ask* your brother where he is.'

Igorik stared at her. 'What are you talking about?'

'You could use his dreams to reach him.'

'I can't make myself go to his dream. It happens without either of us doing anything.'

'That may be so, but perhaps it can be invoked

deliberately if the need is strong enough.' She was certain that with her help, he could will himself to Red's dreaming mind. Always assuming Red was dreaming at the moment they made the attempt. If they succeeded, they would not only be able to learn his whereabouts; she could review his memory of those who had lately come through the rift.

She held out her hands.

'What are you doing?' Igorik asked with a suspicion that warned her to be very careful.

'You must be entirely in accord with yourself to do this,' she told him in a soothing voice. 'There can be no part of you that does not wish to reach your brother, for such dream travelling as this is dangerous. You could be lost between your dreams and his, if your reach is not very sure. Holding my hand will help us to make common cause.'

She realised from the thoughts floating about her, that Igorik was finding her arguments vague and unconvincing. But as she had calculated, his apprehension for his twin was greater than his concerns about her. He gave her his hands and she told him to close his eyes and think of Red. Then she poured her own dream travelling ability and strength into engaging the power of his premonition.

There was a tug, a moment of nausea and a flight through icy darkness. Then they were standing in the corner of a small, windowless cell. Red was sitting on a chair in the middle of the cell in a circle of greenish light, head in his hands. Igorik stepped forward and lay his hand on his twin's shoulder.

Red looked up, his face tormented. 'I am a fool, Igorik. I walked into a trap! If I could just have kept my head I might have got away, but seeing Iakas …'

'Iakas?' Igorik looked at Katya, 'Is this dream or reality?'

'I don't know,' Katya said, staying in the shadows for fear that Red would recognise that she was not part of his brother and say something that would dislodge her from the dream. 'Maybe it is a nightmare.'

Igorik shook his head. 'No. Red is in danger.' He turned back to his brother. 'Where were you when you saw Iakas?'

'The … the Archon's palace. I saw Rad de La'rel heading there with a messenger. He had just got back from an expedition. I started to tell him what I thought about the fog and he told me to come and explain on the way.'

'The fog?' Igorik echoed.

Red did not seem to hear. 'Rad said he thought I might be right about the fog because his partner Tulcia had been so strange and sluggish when he got back. He had thought she must be ill. Then he said I had better tell my story to the Archon.' Red broke off to groan again.

'Ask him to show us what happened when he got to the palace,' Katya thought at Igorik.

Igorik nodded imperceptibly and said, 'Remember what happened at the palace and I can watch.'

Red gave him a bemused look, then closed his eyes.

Instantly, they were all in a street which Katya recognised as one which ran alongside the Archon's palace. She and Igorik watched as Red and a tall young man followed a blond man whose bent head and servile manner marked him a palace servant of the Archon. Red had merged with his remembered self.

'What now?' Igorik asked.

'We follow them,' Katya said.

They caught up with the three just as they passed through a side gate in the palace wall. There was a Watch post beside the gate, and the guide was visibly startled to find it empty.

'Where are the guards?' His voice floated back to them, sharp with concern.

'I do not know, sir,' the servant answered in a low voice. He led them across an empty courtyard and through a door into a richly appointed, but also empty circular foyer.

The guide stopped and stared about. 'This is impossible. Where are the officials? Other servants? People don't just walk into the palace like this. Attendant, where is the Archon?'

The servant turned, revealing pale grey eyes in a narrow youthful face. Katya stared at the bright blue cloud of light at the centre of his eyes.

'Who are you?' the guide demanded.

The Astarian bowed. 'I am to bring you to the Archon,' he answered. He turned and swept away down a hall leading from the entrance foyer, leaving them to follow. Red and the guide exchanged a look and then hurried after him. The Astarian led them to a room at the far end of which stood an ornate golden throne. The Archon sat upon it, slumped down, his face listless.

'What is the matter with him?' the guide asked. But Red's attention was drawn to a low chaise set against another wall, where a tall, beautiful woman in a long black and green gown was bent over the young roofie, Iakas.

'Rolynna!' The Astarian who had conducted them to the room abandoned his servile manner.

'Master!' The woman started back from the couch with a look of mingled defiance and fear. Katya gaped at the young blond Astarian, unable to believe this could possibly be the Scourge. And yet unmistakable authority radiated from him.

Red was staring at him, too. 'I know you! I took your name when you came through the rift from Ghast. You were the leader of a group of traders.'

The Astarian's thin lips curved in a mirthless smile. 'And so here is another whose memory is impervious to my fog.'

'*Your* fog?' the guide echoed.

Red strode across the room to where Iakas lay. His eyes blazed at the woman. 'What have you done to her?'

The woman gave her answer to the Scourge. 'I merely tasted her dreams, master. Unfogged, they are so potent.'

'I commanded you to learn why she was not affected by the fog. I did not give you permission to taste her. Very soon, I will have need of all the dreams I can consume to ensure that no agents follow us.'

'But master, in tasting her dreams, I learned why she is impervious to the fog. In part it is because she lives atop a high roof that rises above the fog level, and in part it is because she is in love. Positive emotions weaken the fog, as you know.'

The Scourge gave her a look that threatened pain, but the woman merely licked her red lips as if this pleased her in some vile way.

'What do you mean you tasted her dreams?' Red demanded. 'Who are you people?'

The Astarian gave a mocking bow. 'I am Isarda, formerly of the closed world, Astariah. More recently of Ghast.'

Katya felt as if she had been hit in the chest. This was the Scourge then, but how could he look so young?

'You wanted to be taken to the Archon …'

Red's eyes flickered to the Archon who suddenly jerked and spoke.

'The cat has come. We are doomed!' Then he fell back to his morose staring.

The Scourge frowned at him. 'These Quentarans are proving somewhat more resistant than I expected. There is something about this place that strengthens their dreams. These rifts, I suspect.'

'What have you done to the Archon?' the guide demanded. He had shifted his stance and Katya could see from it that he was a warrior in a way that neither Red nor Igorik were, despite their muscular strength.

'He is merely under the sway of my fog. You might say I am saving him for later.' He smiled cruelly.

'Why is Iakas here?' Red grated out the words.

'The girl?' Isarda's voice was indifferent. 'She was asking questions about the fog, so Rolynna brought her here.' He turned to the guide. 'But now to business. You are Rad de La'rel?'

'I am. What is this fog?'

'It is only partly my doing,' the Scourge answered. 'I drink the dreams of a human, leaving despair and indifference. I have merely given these things form and the fog has the marvellous effect of weakening dreams. This makes my task simpler because there is no resistance; unfortunately the dreams are less potent. Very soon I will consume the dreams from all of the humans in this palace, including your precious Archon, and the fog I produce will be enough to kill the dreams of all who dwell in this city. I must ensure that no Quentaran remains alive to tell the tale of our passing to the agents of my world, who will assuredly come seeking me.' Again that cruel smile.

Red looked down at Iakas who was moving in his arms, and noticed a white mark on her forehead where the woman had kissed her. As if she felt the pressure of his gaze, Iakas's eyes flew open and an expression of such anguish came into her face that a fist seemed to enclose his heart and squeeze.

'Iakas,' Red murmured. 'What did she do to you?'

Iakas's eyes sought out the tall woman. 'She was inside my … my head,' she whispered. 'Inside my dreams. She was … Red, she turned into a wolf and everywhere she went, my dreams went dark. I could feel her eating them … I was so afraid. I was calling and calling for you …'

'I am here,' Red said softly, tightening his hold on her.

'… you will teach me to master the ability to travel these wondrous rifts,' Isarda told Rad. The guide's blank expression revealed his fury to Red and he was glad. Rad, angry and in action, was dangerous, and he would swiftly deal with this man and the woman. Then together they would find and dispatch the other three.

'I will teach you nothing,' Rad said flatly.

'Oh, but you will,' Isarda said. 'Once I begin swallowing your dreams you will do anything to stop me. You will beg and weep. You will sacrifice anyone and anything. Of course, I will have to be careful. I have learned from other guides that yours is an art so delicately threaded with dreams and memories that the loss of a single one can mar that ability.'

Rad's face grew more still. 'If you have harmed any other guide …'

'Oh, not too many,' Isarda said lightly. 'Once I realised that they needed their dreams to negotiate the rifts, I decided to seek out the best. That, so I was told, is you.'

'I won't help you,' Rad said.

Isarda smiled. 'Sleep on it.' He lifted his hands.

'We have to stop them,' Igorik announced.

Katya felt his agitation and prayed he would not wake. It had been a feat to keep him asleep after they had been expelled suddenly from Red's memory dream of the events leading up to the moment the Scourge had rendered him and the guide unconscious. She must speak quickly now because this was the only way she could communicate with Igorik, and there were things that must be said.

'If Isarda really means to drain the dreams of so many, he will want them close to where he plans to use them.'

'The caves …' Igorik murmured.

'He cannot be permitted to escape,' Katya voiced her own thoughts without meaning to, but fortunately Igorik did not register her words.

'We have to stop him,' he said. 'That woman Rolynna said positive emotions stop the fog.'

'But the Archon and the others taken at the palace will have neither the will nor the wit to think positive thoughts,' Katya said.

'I wasn't thinking of them. But there are the roofies waiting at Iakas's roost. And everyone who lives in Lower Quentaris. I can get Ma Coglin to help me gather them at the caves.'

'There is no time,' Katya said, the coldness in her heart growing because never had she imagined that she might be forced to use the tiny device embedded in her forearm. It was powerful enough to destroy the rifts and isolate this world forever, killing or at least trapping the Scourge and his followers. She had let them implant it, certain there would never be a need for its use. But she had not known what the Scourge was draining the dreams of worlds. No wonder he had tipped the balance on Caris. A world without dreams was a dead world.

And the dream stealing was not just a means of gaining power. She had seen that from the drunken pleasure Rolynna had taken in her theft of Iakas's dreams. And in the stunning youthful appearance of the Scourge.

'What do you mean there is no time?' Igorik asked suddenly, turning to look at her. Before Katya could think what to say, his face changed and she realised too late that he had noticed that her eyes were the same as those of the Scourge and his followers.

'You are one of them, aren't you?' he snarled. 'A filthy thief of dreams.'

Katya screamed as she was thrust violently from his mind.

Red woke.

He was in a cell and Iakas lay beside him, her head on his lap. He was glad that his nightmare had not awakened her to the worse nightmare of reality. If only it were just a bad dream that they were prisoners of Isarda and his foul dream vampires. His sole hope lay in the unexpected appearance of Igorik in his dream. Because it was clear that Igorik had come to his dream deliberately and was trying to figure out where he was. Unfortunately, given what he had told his twin, Igorik would go to the Archon's palace.

Through the bars of the cell, Red could see two of Isarda's people. A man who sat motionless and an older woman who prowled endlessly back and forth in the space between the cells, wringing her hands and occasionally coming to the bars to sniff, her red-centred eyes glowing with hunger. In other cells Red could see officials and guards and servants, all standing or sitting with the same vacant expressions and blank eyes as the Archon. Fogged but so far unharmed. There had been more originally but they had been led away in small groups to the rift caves. That was apparently where Isarda would consume their dreams in order to gain the power he needed to turn the fog into a weapon to use on all of Quentaris.

Red didn't know what was to happen to him or Iakas, save that Isarda had commanded no one was to touch them but him, on pain of death. Red had the horrible feeling that they were being saved for the master's private consumption, like some rare mead.

Rad had been taken elsewhere, presumably so that Isarda could torture the knowledge he needed from the guide.

'He won't give you what he wants,' Red said aloud.

But Iakas moaned and he wondered, with a stab of fear, exactly how many dreams had been stolen from her.

8

Difficult Choices

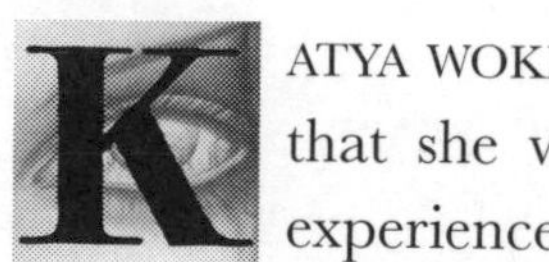

KATYA WOKE AND WAS horrified to discover that she was caged. For a moment she experienced such terror she could neither see nor hear. She forced herself to calmness and realised the cage was standing on the step of Igorik's hovel.

She heard a soft miaow and saw Orb and another bigger cat behind her, prowling back and forth in the shadows. This must be the cat she had promised to bring, whose mistress had been killed by the Scourge. There was time for a brief exchange before Igorik grabbed up the cage and set off. Then she heard a voice.

'You sure she not cat?'

It was Igorik's drainer partner, Vrod. She recognised the voice.

'Very sure,' Igorik said. 'She's one of them and she's a shape-changer. I figured it out from what Iakas said about that woman turning into a wolf before she ate her dreams.'

'You sure she one of them?' Vrod asked.

'I said I was sure,' Igorik said heavily.

Katya miaowed desperately, willing him to let her out so that she could transform and explain. Her superiors had forbidden her to take on her human shape, but matters had gone too far now.

Igorik had either not heard her miaows or was ignoring them. She guessed the latter. Too late to wish she had told him the truth sooner. It occurred to her only now that she had kept him in the dark and had used him just as her superiors had done to her.

Now she was paying for her mistake.

'Why cat girl come to you?' Vrod asked.

'I don't know,' Igorik said through clenched teeth, 'I guess she thought I was my brother. A guard who could be useful.'

'How she make mistake?' Vrod asked after another few minutes. 'Animals smell good. Smell better than humans can smell.'

'I don't know,' Igorik said tersely.

'She eat your dreams?' Vrod asked a few steps later.

'No!' Igorik snarled.

'Why her no eat?' Vrod asked after some more steps.

'I don't know,' Igorik shouted. He glared down at the cage and Katya looked into his eyes and miaowed a song to ask his forgiveness; to beg him to let her out.

Please, she sang.

'What you doing to cat?' Vrod demanded, wincing.

'I'm not doing …' Igorik suddenly stopped, threw his cloak aside and slammed the cage on the ground, jarring Katya's teeth together. He opened the side of the cage with one flick of his hand, drew his sword from his belt and stood back.

Igorik stared as the little grey cat emerged from the cage. She looked up at him then crept under his cloak. The cloak bulged and humped up and suddenly there stood the girl of his dreams, his cloak wrapped around her.

'Igorik, I am so sorry,' she said, and there was a pleading note in her voice. 'I should have told you the truth but at first I didn't think you would believe me, and then I was just too involved in ...'

'What are you doing here?' Igorik interrupted in a hard voice.

She straightened and her tone changed. 'I am an agent of Astariah sent to learn the whereabouts of the criminal shape-changer, Isarda and his companions. I was ordered to retain my cat form because once I took my human form, Isarda would have known I was here and he would have fled through a rift. His crime was too terrible for us to risk losing his trail. The only way I was able to communicate with anyone here was to dream merge.'

'You did not think to warn us?'

'I was forbidden in case the Scourge were to be alerted. My superiors did not expect him to begin killing. It was believed that Isarda would seek to master the ability to negotiate the rifts, so that he could travel to endless worlds. I was commanded to find him and return to let other agents come to deal with him. They could not come sooner because they could not remain in beast form as long as I can, and once they took on their human shape, Isarda would know of their arrival.'

'What Scourge do bad?' Vrod asked.

Katya looked at the troll. 'He destroyed a world, Vrod. Not just the human life on it, but all life. He sucked away the dreams of the people of that world until the balance shifted from life to death. If he leaves here with the secret of rift travel, he will do that to other worlds. Countless other worlds. And you see how young he looks? His crime is keeping him young.'

'He is immortal?' Igorik asked.

'I think he will become so,' Katya said. 'I have to stop him.'

'How?' Vrod asked. 'You fight him?'

'There is now only one thing I can do and that is to destroy the rifts so that he cannot go through any of them. I have … a sort of magical device with me that can …'

'No!' Igorik cried.

Katya stepped back from him, holding up her

hands. 'I can destroy the rifts right now, but if I do that here, the city and all of its inhabitants will die. Let me go to the caves then the city will be safe.'

'The rifts *are* Quentaris,' Igorik said.

'I am truly sorry,' Katya whispered. 'You must understand that I have no choice.'

'You do have a choice. If we can get everyone whose mind is unfogged to the rift caves, we can stop him.'

'There is not time enough. The moment I took my human form, Isarda knew that an Astarian agent was in Quentaris.'

'He will think you've only just come through! He won't realise you've been here for days and days and know what he is planning. It will take him time to get all of those people from the palace to the caves.'

Before Katya could answer, pain cleaved through Igorik's head and he lifted both hands to his head and gave a great cry of pain. 'Red!'

Katya stepped forward and put her hands on either side of his face, forcing him to look at her. 'Isarda is trying to consume him. He will be unconscious. You must let me inside your mind so that I can reach him. That is the only way I can protect him.' She looked sideways at Vrod. 'Igorik has to be asleep.'

'Asleep,' Vrod said, and lifted his club.

Igorik found himself standing in darkness. He heard Katya's voice calling him, but it seemed far away. He knew that she was seeking entrance to his mind, but something in him would not open to her. He decided he must try to reach Red himself, before it was too late.

He let himself feel the premonition pulsing through his mind, far stronger than ever before. He let it drag him from his dream. There was the rush of freezing darkness and then he was in the same cell, but now Red was standing against the wall, his arms chained to a ring set into the stone. The chains glowed green and black and were cutting into his arms.

Isarda stood facing Red. 'You cannot refuse me, human. It amuses me that you try.'

'Then why haven't you drained my dreams already?' Red demanded.

'Because I wish your friend the guide to have time to understand what will happen if he does not agree to aid me. It turns out to be fortunate that you accompanied him. Torturing you will be an even more effective way to force him to give me what I need.'

'He won't help you,' Red grated the words out. 'He will know that you will kill me *and* him when you have got what you want from him.'

'Oh, I think you misjudge the power of human friendship. He will not be able to bear his friend in pain. And of course there is always the foolishness of human hope which seems able to thrive under the most ludicrous conditions.'

'He won't help you no matter what you do to me,' Red said.

'If you are correct, I shall have the pleasure of consuming your dreams then I will finish what Rolynna began with your pretty little friend. Let us see if your tough companion can withstand the screams of a woman …'

'Swine!' Red grated and strained against the chains binding him.

Isarda laughed. A hideous sound, for there was not the slightest bit of humour in it. 'You cannot withstand me.'

'*He* might not be able to,' Igorik said quietly.

Isarda swung round to look at him with mild

surprise. 'You have summoned up a dream alter ego. How very amusing.' But then his expression changed. 'Ah no. Remarkable. It is another dreamer. You have a dream link with … what? It must be close. A brother? Ah, I see. Twin brothers. Let us see if heat will help you to mind your own business, human.' He stepped towards Igorik and lifted a long-fingered hand. A livid greenish light haloed out from his fingers and Igorik reeled back with a hiss of pain.

Dimly, he seemed to hear Katya calling to him. Saying something, but he did not know what it was.

'You do realise that I can drain *your* dreams while you are here?' Isarda said.

'Get out!' Red cried. 'Igorik, please don't play the hero this time!'

'I will not leave you to him,' Igorik snarled, resisting Red's weak attempts to expel him. Again he was aware of Katya. Begging him to open, but the bit of him that was closed to her would not give way.

All at once he seemed to feel her hands on his face and … was it her lips on his?

… dreamers can control their dreams … he heard her voice clearly inside his mind. He shook his head and the shocking feeling of her mouth on his faded.

Isarda lifted his hands and again the unhealthy green light blazed out. Igorik stifled a cry of pain and in that second understood what Katya had been trying to tell him. He turned sideways to where Red watched with horrified eyes.

'You can control this. It's your dream. Trust me and just will … argh!' This time he could not help crying out at the heat of the strange green fire.

Then all at once he was holding a sword.

He gaped at it in disbelief and heard Red's incredulous, triumphant laughter. 'How about a flaming sword?'

A blinding white fire ran over the face and keen edges of the blade, lighting every cranny in the walls of the dingy cell. Isarda flinched back from the radiance. But then he stopped and laughed. That vile meaningless scrape of sound became a roar of defiance and rage as he transformed into a monstrously huge black lion. He feinted a slash at Igorik, then turned on Red who pulled as far back as his bonds would let him from those killing claws and teeth.

'Red!' Igorik cried. 'This is a dream! You can will yourself free just as you willed this sword to me. We're only visitors here! Isarda used the fog to stop people feeling hope and having the sense to figure this out.

To stop anyone realising they could fight him!'

Red gave a great cry and the chains dropped away. Then he, too, bore a weapon. His sword did not flame, but was transparent and sparkling as if formed of diamond. He came to stand beside Igorik and threw his twin a look of elation. They both turned to the lion.

It vanished.

Igorik opened his eyes to find Katya bending over him, her gold-centred grey eyes swimming with tears. 'You are safe!' she said.

'I … I heard you,' Igorik whispered. *I felt you,* he wanted to say. But she was getting to her feet.

'Isarda will take the guide with him now. He has no other choice. I must go to the caves.'

'Wait as long as you can,' Igorik said, praying that Isarda would be in too much of a hurry to kill Red out of revenge.

Katya drew a long breath. Then she nodded, and her dark hair swung in a curtain, covering her expression. 'All right …' Then she straightened. 'Red is being kept in the Halls of Justice.'

'Of course. The cell,' Igorik muttered. 'But how did you know?'

'A cat told me. I have had them seeking Isarda and one of them happened to follow his mistress back to the place she had been lured, and killed. I recognised the description as being the Halls of Justice. I think his mistress might have been the woman you found in the drain.' Before Igorik could say a word to all this, Katya transformed, leapt from his crumpled cloak and vanished into the shadows.

Igorik turned to the troll. 'Vrod, you have to help me ...'

'I won't help you,' Rad had said.

'Let us see if this will change your mind,' Isarda had responded silkily. Then he had bent to press his thin lips to Red's forehead in a foul parody of a kiss. Red had groaned and twice since he had called out his twin's name. Watching, Rad had fought against weakening, knowing such creatures as these had not honour enough to keep any bargain.

Then Iakas awoke and began to scream. 'Stop him. He is eating Red's dreams!' Her terror had been so great that it shook his resolve not to give this monster what he desired.

But now, suddenly and shockingly, Isarda staggered back with a cry. The woman Rolynna rushed to him, and he struck her. Then his expression grew cold and urgent. 'An Astarian agent is here. I felt them arrive even as I was within the dream of this fool. We must get to the rift caves immediately.'

'But master, you do not know the secrets of rift travel yet,' Rolynna cried.

'We will take the guide and go through any rift. Once elsewhere, I will learn what we need to know. Bring the girl in case the guide needs persuading.'

'What about the man?'

Isarda glanced indifferently at Red's unconscious form, then he said, 'Forget him. He will die soon enough with all of the rest here.'

Iakas fought when they were leaving, but at a wave of Isarda's hand she crumpled, unconscious again. One of the male shape-changers threw her over his shoulder, asking, 'What of the agent? He may be at the rift caves.'

'I doubt it for he cannot know yet what is happening here. How many are there ready to be drained?'

'Less than a quarter of those gathered in the cells,' the other said. 'Too few to produce a fog that would kill the dreams of an entire city.'

'Then we will concentrate on the guides,' Isarda said. 'I will direct the fog. But now let us go.'

Rad did not struggle when the woman pushed him before her. Perhaps if Isarda had been under less pressure, he might have wondered at that. But maybe he thought the guide feared him. All the better, for Rad had a plan that required Isarda to underestimate him. He meant to pretend to give in at the last moment, claiming to fear passing blind through a rift. He would offer to lead them then beg to leave Iakas behind, claiming there were too many to be led safely. Then he would guide them to one of those worlds that guides knew and steered clear of. He would lead them there and away from the opening so that it would be too late for retreat when the beasts appeared. He would die too, of course, but one life was a small price to pay to stop Isarda.

Outside, he walked calmly through the coiling mist, regretting only that he would not see Tulcia again. But she would understand. Nobody understood him better than she did.

It did not take them long to reach the nearest rift caves. The streets were deserted and Rad wondered at how he had not realised something was drastically wrong when he had come out of the caves that morning to find the city so very empty. But when he arrived home he had been preoccupied with Tulcia who had been lying on her bed fully clothed. Before he could do more than wonder if she was ill, Isarda had knocked at the door, parading as a messenger from the Archon.

The Scourge stopped abruptly.

In the gate through which all rift travellers must pass to reach the caves was a small grey cat seated on a bundle of white rag. Before anyone could speak, it transformed with an oddly discomfiting shimmer into a young woman who pulled the rags about her and tied them unhurriedly about her neck. Then she shook back a fall of silky dark hair and turned grey eyes on them. Rad saw with a sinking heart that her eyes were the same as those of Isarda and his foul minions.

But instead of bowing to her master, the girl said in a clear, calm voice, 'In the name of Astariah, I command that you surrender yourselves to me.'

'*You* are the agent?' Isarda sounded disbelieving.

'They sent a kitten?'

The girl ignored this. 'I will not allow you to pass.'

'*You* will not allow?' Isarda laughed. 'You have not the means to stop me. I will destroy you with the power of the fog.'

'The moment you seek to gather up the energy left in the fog, I will enter the caves and destroy the rifts. You may believe that I have that power.'

Rad did not doubt it. There was something implacable in the young agent's face. He heard the woman Rolynna suck in a breath of air.

'If you destroy the rifts, you will die with the knowledge that you have left these humans to my mercy. Do not imagine that a single one of them will be left with a dream when I am done with them.'

'Oh, I think we have shown you how capable we are of defending our dreams,' said a familiar voice. 'Now let us show you how we will deal with your fog of despair.' Rad turned his head to see Red and his twin brother Igorik approaching the rift wall. Behind them was a motley crowd of street flotsam and roofies, and in the midst of them stood the fat and formidable Ma Coglin.

'Come on, you mangy flotsam,' she bellowed, albeit somewhat breathlessly. 'We will show these scum how even the lowest in Quentaris have the courage to fight for their dreams!'

To Rad's astonishment, the fog really did seem to thin about them. From the corner of his eye, he saw Red circling round towards the man who had Iakas slung over his shoulder. Igorik came nearer to Isarda, but when he spoke it was to the young agent.

'You see, Katya? There is no need to destroy the rifts to stop him,' he called to her.

Rad could not imagine how he knew her name.

'Stay back, Igorik!' the girl cried, sounding alarmed. 'Remember the Scourge is a shape-changer!'

'Ah,' Isarda said with sudden triumph. 'I wonder what your superiors would say to your becoming the pet of a human, little cat? And I think, after all, that you might not find it so easy to destroy the rifts that mean so much to your muscular and extremely irritating friend. Maybe we will just take the chance and escape.'

'No!' This time there was real fear in her voice. 'I will destroy the rifts and you with them, if you try to go through.'

'No Katya!' Igorik shouted.

'I have a duty …' the girl said desperately. She

was backing towards the caves now, her attention on the big drainer. Isarda suddenly turned to his minions and hissed at them to change shape and flee into the caves.

'I will deal with the agent.'

'Watch out!' Rad warned, but even as he voiced the warning, Isarda transformed into the biggest, blackest lion he had ever seen and leapt towards the girl. Rad was toppled sideways, and with no hands to steady himself, he fell hard to the cobbles. He found himself looking at the unconscious Iakas, who lay beside him on the ground. Rad struggled to turn so that he could see what was happening, heart in his mouth for if the agent did have a way to destroy the rifts, this was when she would do it.

But not only were the cliffs intact when he managed to turn over, the enormous lion and the wolves into which Isarda and his followers had transformed had stopped short of the rift caves. At first he thought the agent must have some magical weapon trained on her quarry, but no. Her body lay slumped on the rough ground too. Rad could not see if she was dead or merely unconscious, but he must be concussed because he seemed to see two cats winding about her still form.

But why weren't the shape-changers making good their escape?

It wasn't until Red hauled the guide unceremoniously to his feet in order to get to Iakas, that he saw what was happening. In every cave entrance visible from where they were stood trolls, all of them broad-shouldered and powerful despite their short stature, and all with clubs and cheerfully ferocious expressions.

'You see,' Igorik said to Isarda. 'There are caves below the rift caves, and fissures leading up from them. But of course you probably didn't discover that, seeing as how you were so busy with other matters. Now, you *could* still try to escape, but I should warn you that trolls eat their prisoners. We, on the other hand, will simply hand you over to your own people.'

9

Aftermath

'SO SHE WENT BACK?' Red asked for the sixth time.

Igorik nodded, busily stirring at a peculiar-smelling greenish mass in the pan.

'Strange to think we were in so much danger from fog,' Iakas said, sipping at the mug of drink she had wisely made herself.

Red could hardly believe they were visiting Igorik

together. When Iakas suggested it, he had been amazed given that she usually disdained even a roof over her head. Igorik had barely seemed surprised when they arrived. *Holding hands.* Red suppressed the urge to smile idiotically at the thought and thanked the spirits that watched over Quentaris and kept it lucky, that the loss of some of her childhood dreams had not cut Iakas too deeply. Katya had explained to them that a certain number of dreams could be lost without harm, because new dreams were always being born. It was only when too many dreams were taken or lost or destroyed without being replenished, that there was any real danger. The thought of what might have happened to Iakas still haunted him. He never wanted to let her out of his sight again. But he knew he couldn't protect her from life. She wouldn't have it and he liked her as she was. A little wild. A little prickly.

The conversation with the Astarian girl had taken place as they waited for Rad to return with other agents from Astariah, who had soon captured their quarry. For of course Isarda and his followers had fled, faced by the trolls. As Igorik had gambled, Isarda was too arrogant to have bothered learning enough about Quentaris to know that there were far too few trolls to guard all of the thousands of cave entrances.

Rad had gone to Ghast because Katya's injuries had meant she was unfit to travel through the rift. Isarda, lion-formed, had opened up deep gashes in her arm and shoulder which had bled so profusely that for a time, there had been some fear that she would die. Red had a fleeting memory of Igorik's agonised expression when he discovered her lying in a pool of blood by the gap in the rift wall, two stray cats licking tenderly at her face.

But when she had gone to the rift to leave with the other Astarians and their prisoners, there had been no more sign of her injuries. Only a sliver of white bandage showing at the cuff of the silken gown the Archon had provided, along with a mass of other finery which the young agent had seemed bemused to receive. She had been more pleased, she had told them, when the Archon had commissioned a statue of a cat in her honour, after publicly rescinding the ban on stray cats. Felines were now to be protected in Quentaris, in honour of the young shape-changer who had crossed the Archon's path with the power to destroy Quentaris, but had refrained from unleashing it.

'What I keep wondering is,' Red said aloud, 'did she choose not to destroy the rift caves, or did she get knocked out *before* she could do it?'

'What does it matter?' Igorik grunted.

'Oh, skyfire!' snapped Iakas. 'Honestly, you men! If she *chose* not to do it, it was because you asked her not to. Which means she cares for you. Which you would have noticed already if you were not blind and stupid into the bargain. Even that vile Isarda saw it!' She shot Red a scalding look as if he were to blame, and he had too much sense to try defending himself.

Igorik was still stirring his pan. 'Don't you two have something to do?' he muttered.

'Plenty,' Red said decisively, thinking about a long overdue rooftop rendezvous. With the fog gone, it was going to be a full moon. He held out his hand to Iakas who set her mug down with a sigh and got to her feet.

Left alone, Igorik gave up the pretence of cooking and sat heavily in his chair, thinking of his last conversation with Katya.

'You should have told me the truth right from the start,' he had told her. Partly it was embarrassment at remembering that he had undressed and bathed in front of her, but mostly it had been finding her covered in blood and thinking she was dead that had made him so angry. He had been afraid for her. Afraid and helpless, just as he had been that dreadful unthinkable day, when he had climbed the potions factory stacks in search of Oleg.

For the first time he let himself remember finding Oleg sitting atop the larger smoke stack, half obscured by greenish purple haze. He had thought at first that it must be a particularly delicious potion being brewed to get him up into such a horribly dangerous position, but then Oleg had turned to him and Igorik had seen the emptiness in his eyes and face. The strange desolation that he suddenly realised he had seen many times leering out from the jokes and manic good cheer. He had tried to talk him down to the platform, but Oleg had shaken his head and without a word of explanation, jumped. In that final moment before he had fallen from view, his face had been the face of the woman whose body Igorik had found in the drains. The face of one whose dreams were dead. For Oleg there had been no dream vampires though. Only a sickness of the heart that had opened up a grey void into which he had fallen. Oleg's mother, he now realised, had been trying to tell him that after her son's death. But he had shut her explanation and the death and even Oleg himself in a dark closet in his mind, along with, he realised, a great part of himself as well.

Until Katya had come, invading his dreams, forcing him to see things he did not want to see; to ask questions he did not want to ask; to feel things he did not want to feel.

He thought of what she had said to the Archon before she had gone back through the rift, when he asked why the loss of mere dreams had been fatal to those who had been victims of the shape-changers.

Dreams are not mere, my lord, she had said gravely. *The very shape of our dreams defines us. We learn about the world and try out our thoughts and visions in them. Our dreams goad us and drive us and summon and sustain us and when we are old, they comfort us. Magic is a kind of dream, and love is a dream, and hope is a dream. Without our dreams, there is no sweetness, no purpose to life.*

And wasn't that what he had allowed himself to become? A man with no dreams? He had not permitted himself to wish for anything and his life reflected that. Even the friendship with Vrod had been something he never allowed himself to think of as more than a working relationship. And Red … hadn't he pushed his twin away as hard as he could? It was only the magic link of twinship that would not let him sever the brother bond.

He thought of Katya. Her long curtain of black hair, her dove-grey eyes with the feathery golden centre, her courage when she had faced Isarda. A wave of longing tinged with pain swept through him at the knowledge that he had let her go. But he did not repress the image. It took courage to dream, and even more courage to dream an impossible dream. Because it *was* impossible to see her again. Her world was a closed world and now that she had returned along with the other agents and their prisoners, there was no way to reach her nor even to get a message to her.

Or was there a way? The question came to him that night on the verge of sleep, like the touch of a needle that pricks without piercing the skin. Because dreams were not like worlds that could be closed. Their boundaries could be crossed by determined dreamers, so long as there was a link. And there *was* a link between him and Katya. He thought of that ghostly kiss, and was sure of it.

When at last he slept, he dreamed that he was

searching for something in the caves beneath Quentaris. The very caves from which rose the fissures the trolls had used to reach the caves nearest the opening in the rift wall. The thought of the trickery that had defeated Isarda made Igorik think of Katya.

And all at once he knew he was dreaming. Knew what he was seeking.

He summoned a vision of her as he had last seen her, walking into the rift cave. He willed himself after her, but strive as he might, there was only a bleak cold into which he hurled his mind over and over, finding no answering spark. No light or warmth to draw him. Perhaps she was too far away. Or she might have closed off the link. Or maybe he had done it, for he remembered how she had been unable to get fully inside his mind to help Red.

He could not bear to think that *he* had broken the link between them. Frustration and desperation made him throw his mind out, spending so much energy that he realised too late he had nothing left to return with. The chill darkness seemed to grow heavier and more cold about him, and motion slowly ceased.

Something dragged at him and without any sense of transition, he found himself in a large room with curved white walls and a gently arching roof. There was a round window in the wall through which lay a blazing blue ocean stretching away to a distant sea horizon. He heard a movement and turned to see Katya in her human form. Her dark hair loose and damp as if fresh-washed, her toes bare under the hem of a long robe of thin cotton that fluttered in the sea breeze.

'What are you doing here?' she asked in a guarded voice.

'Where is here?' Igorik asked, wondering if this might not be his dying dream.

'I am on Astariah and I am sleeping,' she said evenly. 'You are fortunate that I heard you call, for you were lost. You must not now think that because of what happened you can dream travel at any time. It is dangerous to do what you have done.' Her tone was so measured and remote that he found all the things he had wanted to say tangle in his mouth, leaving him mute.

She went on. 'I will send you back to your own mind. But you must not do this again.'

'No!' Igorik cried as she lifted her hand purposefully. 'I don't want to go back yet. I was looking for you. I want to tell you that I … that what you did was … brave.' His voice trailed off lamely.

'Thank you,' she said with a grave courtesy that seemed to push him even further into floundering incoherency. But then something occurred to him.

'How did you hear me?'

For the first time, she looked uncertain. 'I … you called my name.'

'And … you heard it?'

She turned to look out the window at the endless sea. 'There is a link that exists between us. I will break it when I have sent you back.'

That unwillingness of hers to look at him gave him the courage to ask, 'Is that what you want, Katya? To break the connection between us?'

'You were a means to an end,' she said.

'Liar,' Igorik cut her off softly, and suddenly he felt determined and certain of himself. 'If that were true, you would have broken the connection already. And it might not be so easy to break as you think because *I* don't want it broken. In fact, I have every intention of using it to invade your dreams every night until I convince you …'

She turned swiftly, a very cat-like movement, her strange lovely eyes searching his. 'Convince me of what?'

He held her gaze. 'To convince you that when you enter a person's dreams, for whatever reason, you become part of them and they of you. When you entered my dreams, you gave yourself to me, and … I find I cannot bear to lose you.'

It seemed to him that the golden cloud in her eyes thickened. 'It was not just my name you called, Igorik. You called out that you loved me … I thought it must be my longing that made me hear the words.'

'You … longed to hear those words?'

She smiled, a slow sweet smile. 'My cat self knew long before my human self that we belonged together. That is what made me follow you when I first arrived in Quentaris, rather than your brother.'

Joy burst in his heart like fireworks, filling him with heat and brightness. 'Will you … could you think of living in Quentaris? I know I can't come to your world …'

'Indeed you cannot. On the other hand, I believe my superiors would be only too relieved to grant my request to depart Astariah. There is just one problem.' Her words were serious, but there was a feline glimmer of mischief in her face. 'I am part cat and it is common knowledge that you have a terrible aversion to cats.'

And so easily and suddenly his arms were around her. 'Who said I don't like cats?' he growled. 'I *love* cats!'

Without warning she transformed. He bent at once and scooped the little grey cat gently into his arms, lifting her so that she could press her small soft head and ears against the underside of his chin. Marking him as her territory. Then she curled against his chest as if she could hear the soft thunder of his heart, and began to purr …

THE QUENTARIS CHRONICLES

Swords of Quentaris

Paul Collins

Rad de La'rel is a street urchin who yearns to be a guide to adventurers in the rift caves of Quentaris. But before he can claim his birthright, he must escape the Thieves' Guild and the notorious Vindon Nibhelline with the help of his friend Tulcia. Only then will he be proclaimed the greatest guide since his ancestor, the legendary Nathine de La'rel.

Paul Collins has been short-listed for many Australian science fiction and fantasy awards. He has won the Aurealis, the William Atheling and the inaugural Peter McNamara awards. His books include *The Great Ferret Race, The Dog King, Dragonlinks, Slaves of Quentaris* and *Dragonlords of Quentaris*.

ISBN 0 7344 0470 0

Quentaris in Flames

Michael Pryor

When a fire is deliberately lit in the city of Quentaris, Nisha Fairsight and her minstrel friend Tal investigate and soon uncover a plot threatening its inhabitants. Adding to the city's woes is the threat of invasion from the vicious, insect-like Zolka, who are making it even more dangerous than usual to pass through the rift caves.

Nisha must discover her fire-magic heritage and her place in Quentaris. Will she be able to save the city and her friends?

Michael Pryor is the author of many popular and award-winning novels and short stories, including *Beneath Quentaris* and *Stones of Quentaris*. Michael lives in Melbourne with his wife Wendy and two daughters, Celeste and Ruby.

ISBN 0 7344 0469 7

The Perfect Princess

Jenny Pausacker

Tab Vidler is an orphan who works for the Dung Brigade, sweeping the streets of Quentaris. One day she meets a mysterious stranger called Azt Marossa and before long she is helping him escape from the Archon's guards and avoid Duelph and Nibhelline sword fighters. Most importantly of all, she's finding out what really happened to her heroine, the Perfect Princess, who fled Quentaris years ago …

Jenny Pausacker has written sixty books for young people, from picture books and junior fantasies to science fiction and young adult novels, winning several awards. Jenny's titles include *Scam*, *Looking for Blondie* and *Death by Water* (Crime Waves), and *The Rings* in Lothian's After Dark series.

ISBN 0 7344 0586 3

The Revognase

Lucy Sussex

Life in the city of Quentaris is never dull. The city's two feuding families, the Blues and the Greens, have just held a battle in the market. There has been a duel between wizards and a burglary at the Villains' Guild. And the Chief Soothsayer has just prophesied another disaster: 'I see a disc of changing colours, passing from hand to hand. I see murder, misery and mayhem. I see the disc destroying everyone who touches it!'

Lucy Sussex has been published internationally and in various genres, including children's fiction, literary criticism, horror and crime fiction. She has won the Ditmar and Aurealis Awards, and been short-listed for the Kelly Awards (for crime writing) and the Wilderness Society Environment Award for children's literature.

ISBN 0 7344 0495 6

Beneath Quentaris

Michael Pryor

In the fabled city of magic, mystery and mayhem, young Nisha is struggling to come to terms with her fire-magician heritage. With the help of young minstrel Tal, Nisha learns to control her power while being swept up in events that threaten Quentaris itself, leading her to the fabulous and forbidding underground streets of Lower Quentaris.

ISBN 0 7344 0556 1

Slaves of Quentaris

Paul Collins

Yukin and his mate, Yulen, flee their campsite when Akcarum slave-traders attack. Unable to escape the Akcarum hunter birds, they are caught and transported to Quentaris. On their journey through the rift caves Yukin discovers a power that taps into the senses of insects and animals. But can it save them in time?

ISBN 0 7344 0557 X

Stones of Quentaris

Michael Pryor

Who is stealing the stones of Quentaris? With Quentaris preparing for the annual Carnivale celebration, Jaq Coblin is thrown into an adventure with four mysterious strangers, powerful magic and a horde of barbarians made of sand. What can Jaq do but use his wits and hold on tight?

ISBN 0 7344 0619 3

Dragonlords of Quentaris

Paul Collins

Rad de La'rel is about to sign a trade agreement with the devious Fendonians when he is captured by sky pirates. Sold into slavery, he becomes a pawn to the all-conquering dragon-lords of Udari. When he returns to Quentaris it has been invaded by the very creatures Rad has escaped from. Worse — nearly every citizen is wearing a slave's neck collar.

Can the famous Quentaran rift guide release his people from the grip of the invaders?

ISBN 0 7344 0620 7

The Ancient Hero

Sean McMullen

An ancient stalker prowls Quentaris. He seeks to destroy a powerful book of spells, but must get past the Murderers' Guild, the City Watch, and the City Militia. No one is safe, or so it seems, until a student called Zelder translates the spell that could be the key to his undoing …

Sean McMullen is the acclaimed author of numerous science fiction and fantasy books. He has won a dozen awards, and his work has been translated into eight languages.

ISBN 0 7344 0657 6

Angel Fever

Isobelle Carmody

Ely is the lonely, simple-minded younger sister of one of the Quentaran city guards. She dreams of becoming a fearless rift guide, but knows there is no hope of her dream coming true. Then comes a rain-filled day when she rescues an enormous and beautiful winged man in the rift caves.

From that moment on, nothing will ever be the same for Eely again.

Isobelle Carmody is a prolific science fiction and fantasy writer of many award-winning books. These include *Dreamwalker* and *Journey from the Centre of the Earth.* Isobelle divides her time between Prague in Eastern Europe and her home on the Great Ocean Road in Victoria, and is currently working on the final book in the Obernewtyn Chronicles.

ISBN 0 7344 0689 4

The Mind Master

John Heffernan

Torrad, a young boy working for the Miragho family, possesses strange magical powers of the mind. Through his ability, he has uncovered an evil plot against the people of Quentaris. But can one boy change the course of Quentaran history?

John Heffernan is the author of numerous acclaimed publications including *Spud, Rachael's Forrest, More Than Gold, My Dog* (CBC Book of the Year for Younger Readers and CBC Honour Book in 2002) and *Two Summers* (short-listed for the CBC Picture Book of the Year in 2004). He runs a sheep and cattle property with his wife in northern New South Wales.

ISBN 0 7344 0656 8

Treasure Hunters of Quentaris

Margo Lanagan

Tikko knows that some day she'll be a guide, like her brothers and sisters — but so soon? Lord Eustachio Doro isn't even sure he wants to follow his family's tradition and explore other worlds. Find out what happens when this unlikely pair are thrown together to hunt for treasure in the rift caves near Quentaris. Will they win glory and do their families proud, or fall headlong into disaster?

Margo Lanagan lives in Sydney and is an award-winning author for readers of all ages. *Treasure Hunters of Quentaris* is Margo Lanagan's first contribution to The Quentaris Chronicles. Her work has been short-listed for the Aurealis, Ditmar and New South Wales Premier's awards.

ISBN 0 7344 0690 8

Rifts through Quentaris

Karen R. Brooks

Adyren Worthing longs to be anything other than what she is: an apprentice in the League of Bibliophiles, but master thief does not figure in her daydreams. When she is accused of stealing, no one, not even her own family, believes her claims of innocence. To uncover the truth, she must travel to another world and discover the terrible secret of her birth.

Karen Brooks is a senior lecturer in popular culture at the University of the Sunshine Coast. She is the author of the popular Cassandra Klein series, which includes *It's Time, Cassandra Klein, The Gaze of the Gorgon, The Book of Night* and *The Kurs of Atlantis*.

ISBN 0 7344 0745 9

The Plague of Quentaris

Gary Crew

But on the last night of the Three-Day Dark, some said they saw a shape in the starry sky. A black void, where no star shone. A void in the shape of a rat ...

Is this a warning of fantastical events to befall Quentaris? What part do the rat children, Anton and Vega, play in this horror? Is this the final calamity that will destroy the mighty city?

Gary Crew is one of Australia's most awarded authors, winning the Children's Book Council of Australia Book of the Year award four times. He is internationally acclaimed for his fantasy novels and illustrated books, including the best-selling *Strange Objects* and *The Watertower*.

ISBN 0 7344 0773 4

Princess of Shadows

Paul Collins

Tamaika Erskona works in the Quentaris Library, a labyrinthine building which covers an entire city block. Gifted Tamaika loves books and works hard but is treated like a doormat — bullied and unappreciated by her stepmother, sisters and colleagues.

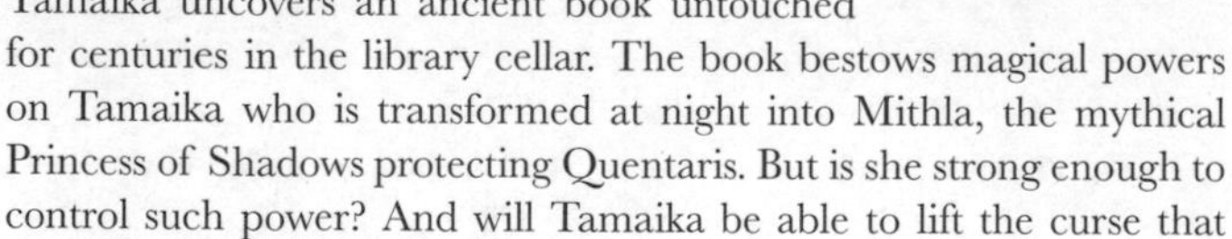

When a dreadful curse descends on Quentaris, Tamaika uncovers an ancient book untouched for centuries in the library cellar. The book bestows magical powers on Tamaika who is transformed at night into Mithla, the mythical Princess of Shadows protecting Quentaris. But is she strong enough to control such power? And will Tamaika be able to lift the curse that turns citizens into stone?

ISBN 0 7344 0799 8

Nightmare in Quentaris

Michael Pryor

Arna Greentower and her business, The Old Tree Guesthouse, are experiencing tough times. Employees mysteriously disappear, deliveries go astray and business is the worst it's ever been. But Arna's foster-daughter Nisha, a fire magician, is determined to save her guardian's business from collapse.

Nisha and her friend Tal seek to uncover the secrets behind the forbidden room and the memory-eating powers of its menacing occupant. But he is only one of Arna's enemies. Former business rival and fugitive Gorv is back in Quentaris to bring Arna down.

ISBN 0 7344 0774 2

The Murderers' Apprentice

Pamela Freeman

Like her father and mother before her, Merrith is apprenticed to become an assassin with the Murderers' Guild. But Merrith is hopeless with a dagger and sword, inept at mixing poison and isn't quite okay with the idea of killing people anyway. Merrith's talents, it seems, lie elsewhere. Just as she is due to begin her apprenticeship, the Soothsayers' Guild instruct Merrith to join an expedition to the rift caves, and it comes with a warning: if she fails to go, Quentaris will be destroyed.

Can Merrith save Quentaris from devious Sorrell, the leader of the expedition? And will she discover her true vocation and escape her supposed destiny as a professional murderess?

Pamela Freeman started writing stories for children in the early 1990s while she was a scriptwriter at the ABC. Her work, which includes *The Willow Tree's Daughter, Victor's Quest* and *Pole to Pole*, has been short-listed for the NSW Premier's Literary Awards, the Children's Book Council Book of the Year Award for Younger Readers and the Koala Awards. Pamela grew up in Sydney's western suburbs and now lives in the inner city with her husband and young son.

ISBN 0 7344 0800 5